To Larry,
Another one of life's
little mysteries.
                    Rich
                    10/94

# Letting
# Blood

# *Letting Blood*

## Richard Platt, M.D.
### and
## Orah Platt, M.D.

St. Martin's Press
New York

Although we have drawn on our own experiences and those of our colleagues in imagining these events and settings, none of the events that appear in this book are real, nor is UHOP, nor are any of the characters.

*Design by Glen M. Edelstein*

Library of Congress Cataloging-in-Publication Data

Platt, Richard.
    Letting blood / Richard and Orah Platt.
      p.   cm.
    ISBN 0-312-02941-1
    I. Platt, Orah. II. Title.
  PS3566.L295L4 1989                      89-30151
  813′.54—dc19

First Edition

10  9  8  7  6  5  4  3  2  1

To our friends and associates, who will find themselves only on this page.

# Acknowledgments

We are especially indebted to our most critical reader and adviser—Alexander Platt.

*The physician today seems athirst for blood. Blood-letting, like wine-drinking, is right enough in moderation, but in excess leads to disaster.*

—Jean Fernel (1497–1558)

*A woman's guess is much more accurate than a man's certainty.*
—Rudyard Kipling (1865–1936)

# Letting Blood

**ONE**

THE RAIN began at dawn. At 9 P.M., Loren Asker, physician and biomedical engineer, left a meeting of the board of trustees of the United Hospitals of Philadelphia. At midnight, he took a left-hand turn a little too sharply onto the Schuylkill Expressway at South Street, and entered the northbound off ramp instead of its southbound entrance. He proceeded three hundred yards through the driving rain before confronting a fully loaded tanker truck. Three hours later, his heart, nestled in an Igloo ice chest, safely negotiated the expressway on its way back to his hospital. The transplant surgery itself began at 4:30. In attendance were two anesthesiologists, three thoracic surgeons, four residents, five nurses, and six technicians. At five o'clock, a brown puddle appeared at the base of the operating room's door frame. At 5:35, Montana's phone rang.

It was one of the surgeons. "I'm doing a transplant in a goddamn sewer. Get your ass in here."

Archer Rush Montana sat up straight in bed, juggling the phone and his copy of *Shikasta,* still attached to the little book lamp. "Do you need help mopping?" Montana was ordinarily more courteous than a boy scout, but cardiac surgeons, especially Maddock (Mad Dog to family, colleagues, and underlings—he had no friends), didn't know the difference and it was therapeutic to talk like them once in a while.

*1*

"If you're not here in ten minutes to check this filth for germs, there's going to be hell to pay."

"Everything has germs. The door isn't sterile, the floor isn't sterile, your puddle can't be sterile. I'll come take a look. Don't get your booties wet."

He put the phone down and turned off the light. Molly pulled the covers over her head and mumbled something about five more minutes. He threaded his way across the bedroom, which like the other rooms in the Montana town house was littered with piles of his medical journals, coloring books, her medical journals, computer magazines, copies of *The New Yorker,* spelling workbooks, *American Rowing* magazines, Hardy Boys mysteries, *Bon Appetit*s, and partly completed *New York Times* crosswords. He identified Whimsy's location by the drumming of his stubby Airedale tail on the floor. All four paws were in the air; the nose was still early-morning dry.

As Montana drove through the rain to the hospital, he was paged to the operating room four times. Four years of medical school, four years of residency and fellowship training in infectious diseases, two years of training in epidemiology, and lots of years on the job were scant preparation for the curveballs that came his way. He was the hospital epidemiologist at the United Hospitals of Philadelphia, commonly called UHOP, a brand-new fifteen-hundred-bed teaching hospital affiliated with three of the city's medical schools, Penn, Jefferson, and Temple. UHOP boasted that it had every kind of sick patient known to man and the staff and facilities to handle them.

Montana's job was to keep these patients and staff from getting and/or spreading infections within the hospital. From his unique vantage point, he saw the minute details of UHOP's complex structure and function, and the successes, failures, and the near misses that were rarely recorded and often unappreciated both by the patients and their doctors. He knew who sipped from the

2

president's Wedgwood tea service, which surgical resident operated in his socks, who gave mouth-to-mouth resuscitation to the child who died of meningitis, and who tipped a bucket of soaking urinals onto the case of gauze dressings during a clumsy tryst in the fifth-floor supply room. He could even recognize the hospital's three species of roaches (possibly a legacy of the merger of three separate hospitals into one new building). He also knew UHOP provided some of the world's best medical care.

Montana pulled his thirteen-year-old Honda Civic (book value—"not listed") into his one-hundred-dollar-a-month parking spot and struggled through the rain across the four blocks of construction sites, sidewalk repairs, and hoagie stands that ringed the hospital's South Broad Street location. He took the elevator down to the operating room level and saw the nervous cluster of five administrators (one per cent of the complete complement). It was not a pleasant sight: five pair of Guccis, eight pinstriped cuffs, and two gentlemen-prefer-Hanes ankles, spattered with brown. Montana's own brown suede Wallabees and brown corduroys provided protective coloration—he blended in beautifully with the muck. A housekeeping crew had built a dam from four dozen towels and were mopping the ooze as it trickled across the threshold. Muddy footprints extended down the hall as far as the eye could see.

In the operating room itself, the atmosphere was business as usual. Tense battlefield talk, and plenty of blood spattered on the surgeons, the equipment, the overhead lights, and the floor. They didn't notice Montana's arrival or his departure.

Montana reviewed the blueprints with A. N. Crowe, senior vice-president of the hospital, and with the chief engineer. They closed the operating rooms on the south side of the building, limited access to the flooded areas, and decided to hold a strategy session with the surgeons in an hour. By the time they finished this discussion, three engineers had bored a hole in the wall of a utility closet to reveal a medium-sized geyser.

"The worst of it is that you haven't seen the worst of it," explained A.N. as she led him to the back stairs. "Let's go to CPD; it's under two inches of water and five million dollars' worth of surgical equipment is contaminated."

The Central Processing Department cleaned and sterilized all of the hospital's equipment. It was two stories underground, immediately below the operating rooms. They arrived to find a high-tech tropical rain forest. It was eighty-five degrees, the air was wet, and dirty water dripped from the ceiling in a dozen places. It streamed down the walls and ran over the surgical instruments that hung on wall-mounted racks. Twenty sopping-wet employees bitched and joked as they moved the slippery surgical steel to a makeshift sorting area for cleaning. The task was staggering, both because of the number of pieces to be cleaned and because most of the usual work area was cordoned off. Babe, the sixty-year-old director of CPD whose usually teased platinum blond hair was plastered down to her head, was bolstering morale, directing traffic, rescheduling work shifts, and contacting other hospitals to use their sterilizers. Catching sight of Montana and A.N., she let a handful of bone chisels sink out of sight in the cloudy dishwater, wiped her wet hands on the front of her wet scrub suit, and pushed the hair out of her eyes with the back of her wrists.

"The real tragedy is that we could have saved most of this stuff if we had moved it when the leak started. But it seemed like all the other leaks, so the night crew just put out the buckets."

"All what other leaks?" Montana asked.

"Ms. Crowe can tell you later. I really need you to tell me how to deal with this stuff. Here's what I've set up so far. We've pulled out the stuff that's a must for today's

**4**

procedures and put it over there." She waved at a line of carts whose flexible side panels were rolled up, exposing metal in various shades of brown. She walked them to three four-by-eight-foot plywood panels on sawhorses. "We're sorting it here into the ones that need rewashing and the others that are still clean and only need sterilizing. Unfortunately, there aren't many of those. We're using the table under this canopy to wrap the washed stuff. We won't be able to use our autoclave until at least ten, so I've arranged for the laundry truck to take the stuff for the early cases to Graduate Hospital. It should be back by eight thirty. If the leak doesn't stop by seven, I'll get plant services to put up another tent over the receiving area so we can start on the big pile. I don't think we'll have to cancel anything."

"What was it exactly you need me to tell you? You've covered everything. How about letting me put on a jump suit and hose down those rib spreaders?"

"How about moving along and getting the OR open again?"

Montana and A.N. left CPD to meet with the surgeons. A.N. filled him in as she walked in front of him along a two-by-twelve plank that served as a temporary bridge through the flooded corridor.

"As Babe said, this isn't the first leak we've had, though it's the worst by far. There are really two problems. Last year, the city excavated to repair a municipal storm sewer that goes past our front door. Unfortunately, the fix only lasted a month. During a heavy rain, there's a lot of overflow. That wouldn't be a problem by itself, except that the excavation cracked our foundation seal, so the water seeps in. CPD is the hospital's lowest point, so it's taken the brunt of the seepage. Since the ORs are right above, they're the next to go when the rain gets heavier. We've been negotiating for the past year with the city, the architect, and the builder, but we haven't made

5

any real progress, except that everybody's promising to see everybody else in court. The only thing I've learned from all of this is never to let Freestone tell me where to put my operating rooms."

Freestone, the architects of the new United Hospitals building, was one of the country's foremost firms. Unfortunately, UHOP was its first hospital, and the firm's lack of expertise in medical design became more apparent with every passing day. The list of design flaws was enormous, but the underground operating theaters, located far away from the intensive care units and other support services, ranked near the top.

Their next stop was the surgeons' lounge. The transplant over, the surgical team sat around in their dirty scrubs, feet in assorted clogs, oxfords, and blood-tinged Nikes propped up on the low oval table littered with half-filled Styrofoam coffee cups, saltines, and a couple of jars of peanut butter and jelly with smeary-handled knives balanced across their tops.

In addition to replaying the highlights of the procedure, they didn't know what to make of having held Asker's heart in their hands. They had all known him because he ran UHOP's artificial-heart team. He was a straddler who had combined an ordinary engineering degree from Drexel with an unexceptional degree in medicine from an offshore medical school, and had jumped on the implantable heart bandwagon after the Barney Clark extravaganza in Salt Lake City. Like the others in his field, Asker had taken plumbing to new heights. He could keep a calf alive forever but wasn't close to making a pump that could fit inside a person's chest and also leave space for other essentials, such as lungs. Montana had followed the progress of the work, mostly because he figured that if Asker or one of his competitors ever pulled it off, the recipients of the hardware would be sitting ducks for all sorts of infections. A fundamental problem with bioprostheses was that the human body didn't have the faintest idea how to respond when they became infected. Which they did with discouraging regularity. In general, the bigger the implant, the more likely the infection. Artificial heart valves were problem enough. The implantable heart might prove to be the Hospital Epidemiology Employment Act of the nineties.

Montana was struck by a special irony. One of the major arguments for developing an implantable heart was the fact that there would never be enough human heart donors to meet the need. People didn't come equipped with spare parts. But here was one of the foremost proponents of the mechanical solution dealing a double blow to the field. First by absenting himself from it, and then by easing the demand.

Maddock turned and snarled: "Montana, my patient better not get infected from that crap. How long has it been getting into my OR? It must have caused all those infections we had last month."

Montana went to the refrigerator and poured himself a cup of Tropicana. He let pass the opportunity to comment on Maddock's sudden ability to remember infections that last month he insisted either hadn't occurred ("The incision's just a little weepy."), or weren't serious ("He did fine after we took him back to the OR for a little cleaning up."), or weren't his fault ("That Pronestyl knocked his white count all to hell. It's no wonder."), or all of the above.

"Actually, it's ordinary South Philly mud," Montana explained. "It never got near your patient, and the bacteria in it can't fly through the air. Engineering will check the ventilating ducts and the ceiling panels to see if they've collected any water. The air's filtered just before it enters the room, so it should be all right. As long as water doesn't drip onto the operating table, there isn't any risk to your patients. We won't learn anything from cultures.

Don't use the room again until the leak stops and the room is cleaned."

Mad Dog started to foam at the mouth (that characteristic bubble of saliva was the basis of his nickname). "I'm not setting foot in there until you culture that room."

"My pleasure. We should have the results in two days. You can furlough your staff until then." Montana banked his crumpled cup into the trash can as he turned to leave.

It was easier to do meaningless tests in these situations than to try to educate. These cultures meant hours of extra work for Montana's team and for the staff of the Microbiology Lab. It was no consolation that Maddock would be more inconvenienced than anyone else by the unnecessary loss of the room for two days. During that time, he would ordinarily perform six major operations in that room, netting approximately fifteen thousand dollars in fees. Maddock might be regretting his decision by now, but he'd never admit it.

It was 7:30. The one saving grace of this early morning's adventure was that Montana was starting the rest of his day on schedule.

WHEN MONTANA wasn't lecturing, teaching, traveling, or putting out fires, he started the day at one of the hundreds of computer terminals scattered around the hospital, as he logged on to check for messages. Then he rounded on his hospitalized patients. On Wednesdays, he attended the weekly Infectious Disease conference.

This week a visiting professor was in town, so the interns presented cases for him to discuss. They provided information in stages about each patient's symptoms, physical examination, and laboratory tests, so the discusser could go through the thought process aloud for the audience. This continued until all of the teaching value had been extracted and he arrived at a diagnosis. The discussion of a single case could take an hour, depending on the complexity of the problem and the amount of participation by the audience. Montana had helped choose the cases for this conference so that they fell within the man's area of expertise. He also made clear to the house staff that the purpose of this particular conference was to allow a distinguished visitor to show his stuff. Unfortunately, UHOP interns couldn't resist playing "Stump the Stars." Their presentations were technically perfect. They laid out the patients' histories logically and supplied all of the pertinent data, but they avoided any verbal or body language that gave a hint of the correct diagnosis. Worse, they included enough irrelevant history to obscure the correct diagnosis in a forest of possibilities. Whenever the poor man came anywhere close to penetrating the thicket and closed in on the correct diagnosis (cryptococcal meningitis in this case), the intern would say something such as, "Did I mention that his cryptococcal antigen was negative?" In the end, an intern with the face of a cherub convinced a man with a national reputation for research on cryptococcal meningitis that he didn't know what the patient had, but there was virtually no chance that it was cryptococcal disease.

Midway through the second case, Montana's beeper went off. It was Bella, one of the two epidemiology practitioners who worked for him, and the principal reason that he knew so much about what happened to whom at UHOP.

"Got a minute?" Montana always made a minute when she asked. "Last week's transplant is still in the isolation room in the ICU, so the new guy can't go there. The cardiac team doesn't want him to go to a regular ICU bed. They're afraid he'll get in trouble with the methicillin-resistant staph that was going around the unit last month. I told them we'd found the source and gotten rid of it, but they're skeptical."

"They're a little sensitive just now about infections. Could he stay in the recovery room for a couple of days, while we reculture the patients in the ICU? We were going to do it anyway next week as a check."

"Funny you should suggest that. I just did another set of cultures. They'll be ready day after tomorrow. The recovery room's content to keep him until then unless they get clobbered. They'll call you to referee if space gets tight."

Montana and Bella conferred for another minute and he returned to the conference, where the prof was on the ropes over a chronically swollen foot that belonged to a woman who had walked barefoot in many parts of the world that harbored bizarre fungi. It proved to have a splinter in it.

Montana spent the rest of his morning at a meeting of the hospital's Committee for the Protection of Human Subjects, a group that reviewed the many research projects conducted within the institution. Clinical research had occasioned some of the shining moments in academic medicine, as well as some of the most regrettable, and this committee tried to facilitate the former and prevent the latter. Said another way, the committee made sure that investigators remembered the difference between guinea pigs and people.

It was well past noon when he headed toward his office, which was located three blocks away, unfortunately not in the direction of his parking space. This was another legacy of the new building. The architects had forgotten, or never knew, what support services the hospital required. The Epidemiology Unit's office, like those of the staff of the newborn nursery, the hospital chaplains, and the TV rental service, was discovered, long after the available space had been parceled out, to be missing from the plans. To accommodate all these displaced employees, the hospital bought and renovated a nearby building recently abandoned by a veterinary hospital that had moved out to New Bolton to be nearer the horsey set. Montana shared an office in the Distemper Unit with his staff of two infection-control practitioners and a secretary. They called it Phrygia, after the ancient country in Asia Minor that had been home of Montanism, the ascetic, heretical sect founded in the second century A.D. by Montanus, who claimed prophetic inspiration for himself and his two female associates. The distance to his office did cut down on the number of casual visitors, but that was faint consolation on wet days. Montana put his hip-length raincoat over his knee-length white coat and set out through the rain. Moving fast, he cut a dashing figure.

The Epidemiology staff assembled slowly for its daily meeting. The official beginning of these meetings was 1:30, but it wasn't always easy to tell when idle conversation stopped and business began.

The job of the Epidemiology Unit was to prevent something that most doctors insisted never happens, the spread of infection within the hospital. In fact, every year about two million patients leave hospitals with infections they didn't have when they arrived. They pick up these infections from their physicians during surgery, from equipment that hasn't been cleaned properly, from other patients, from faulty ventilation systems, from contaminated IV solutions, from the germs living on their own bodies, and, especially, from unwashed hands. To Montana, these hospital-acquired, or nosocomial, infections were bad things happening to (mostly) good people. Infections that staff members acquired at work were a parallel concern. Montana's charge was to prevent patients and staff from getting or giving these infections, to track down their sources when they did occur, and to make the hospital look good in the process.

Montana found Bella pacing with her first Diet Coke of the afternoon, as she told Carola about Asker's accident. Bella, who had raised networking to an art form, had already found out more than any formal investigation would ever learn. As far as Montana could determine, she knew all twelve thousand employees at UHOP and communicated with each of them on a daily basis. She loved the thrill of being the first to know and the first to tell. She loved investigating—tracking down rumors, hunting down details. She knew about death, disease, health, birth, conception, and misconception. Gossip was her job description. She loved her job.

Blond, pale, gray-eyed, vaguely waiflike, Carola worked to maintain direct eye contact as she warmed her spiderlike hands around her mug of steaming Red Zinger. Her oddly too-large cellist's thumb nested beneath its handle. Carola was always easily engaged in a human interest story, although surprisingly blasé about gory details—possibly a reflection of her nonprofessional liaison with the lead singer of Trained Attack Dogs.

"Any idea how he got on an off ramp?" Montana was merely keeping up his end of the conversation. Bella was rarely without an idea about anything.

"The trucker *said* you couldn't see anything in the downpour, and it's being listed as a weather-related fatality," she answered, finally sitting down. She obviously didn't put much stock in that explanation.

*12*

"But?"

"But, he must've used that ramp a thousand times. And nobody knows where he was for the couple of hours before that, even though it's only a twelve-minute drive from here. I bet he was having trouble with a honey."

"How about a bottle?" Carola took a simpler view of people's flaws.

Montana allowed that someone must have checked a blood-alcohol level before they took his heart, and he tried to steer them back to something related to business. Like his morning's sojourn in the OR.

As he filled them in on the drippy details of Asker's reincarnation, Montana hung his wet socks over the back of his chair and put his *Times*-stuffed shoes on the radiator. As he rummaged through his green drawstring gym bag for his squash socks and sneakers, he recalled Molly saying he shouldn't rely on athletic gear to bail him out of wardrobe emergencies. He was going to look pretty ridiculous in his red lowtops and grayish (left) and yellowish (right) gym socks. Like the day he broke his glasses climbing through the air vent under the pigeon nest and ended up wearing his shatterproof goggles to sherry hour with the trustees. Or the time they accidentally let the water back into the Jacuzzi tub he was examining, and he found himself lecturing to the second-year medical students in his white coat over his cutoffs and Girls' High T-shirt.

They slowly shifted to the formal review of the day's events. Bella and Carola generally began by describing the new patients with infections and the patients with new infections. They would touch briefly on the type of isolation or precautions they had instituted, and whether there had been any difficulty in getting the hospital staff to cooperate. Although everyone in the hospital agreed with the idea of taking precautions, implementing them occasionally caused problems. This was particularly true

*13*

when infection was suspected but not proven, or when isolation caused a lot of extra work.

For example, about a month ago, Mrs. Cardwell in the B nursery was changing Baby Boy Simpson's diaper when she noticed his umbilical cord stump was a little "soupy." She knew this could be the beginning of a staph infection and obtained a culture. She also knew the baby should be kept apart from the others and handled with gloves for the few days until the cultures were read. But Mrs. Simpson was what the whole evening shift called a worrier (actually she was what they called a screamer). She cried when Baby Boy's Apgar score was only 9 instead of the perfect 10 she'd hoped for. She panicked when his first poop looked like peanut butter. She called the pediatrician at 3 A.M. because she was sure the baby was deaf. She swooned when he lost an ounce on his second day. The nursing staff had spent nearly twenty-four hours a day trying to make Mrs. Simpson realize she had a normal child. Nurse Cardwell knew that precautions and the mere hint of an infection would send Mrs. Simpson off the deep end. She did nothing. Seven days later, all the babies in B nursery had staph belly buttonitis and half were on intravenous antibiotics.

The next topics of discussion were usually problems and potential problems. Dirty needles in the emergency room were certainly a problem. Mountains of used needles and syringes piled up around each bed as patients had blood drawn for tests, pain shots, novocaine injections, tetanus shots, penicillin shots, intravenous hookups, blood transfusions, and, of course, more blood drawn for tests. All this hardware was tossed into open cardboard boxes. The ones that weren't lifted by addicts passing through were always ready to stick an unwary house officer, nurse, volunteer, or housekeeper. The lack of an adequate disposal system was a flagrant violation of regulations and common sense, but years of effort had yielded no progress, largely because cardboard boxes were free. Montana knew the hospital was a sitting duck if OSHA staged a surprise visit, or if one of the hospital's employees filed a complaint.

Bella tried to pay full attention to Montana's soppy story, especially since he seemed to be enjoying himself. But she was too busy thinking ahead about the real bombshell she was about to drop. Montana was winding down. She sat up a little straighter, pulled a manila folder from her Land's End attaché case, recrossed her rather shapely legs, readjusted her short gray flannel skirt, and made it quite obvious that she was next on the agenda.

"New patient, admitted yesterday, healthy fifty-nine-year-old man with community-acquired pneumonia, room 1607." Bella droned on as Carola continued staring at the little yellow taxicab circling the perimeter of her Swatch watch. This was clearly going to be as exciting as Montana's sewer saga. Most pneumonias that people get at home are caused by one of a few viruses or bacteria, turn out to be mild, and resolve without hospitalization. She was just about to ask why the guy had been admitted to the hospital when Bella's well-timed explosion fired.

"His name's Vanning Epps." She looked up from her folder to enjoy the response. Montana shot his sweatband across the room and Carola grabbed the folder as she flashed her "give me a break" eye roll. Epps was one of the fifty wealthiest men in the country and a household word in the business and social columns. A scion of one of Philadelphia's oldest and best-bred families, he had distinguished himself as a college athlete, Rhodes scholar, and progressive businessman. He was a major philanthropist, supporting both local and national charities, and donating his time and effort to a dizzying number of social causes. He was hot: the private jet set, the name on the National Opera House in D.C., the lender of estates to exiled potentates and vacationing presidents.

"Dan Belkins admitted Epps because he also has mild asthma, and Belkins figured the hospitalization was the only way to get Epps away from his paperwork, his associates, and the phone. And he doesn't need special precautions, since he's completely isolated in the V.I.P suite and"—retrieving her folder from Carola, who now hung on every word—"his wife is staying with him, and his taste is definitely preppy," she added, fingering the lapels on her man-tailored blue blazer and smiling at Carola's comparatively hot ensemble featuring a beautifully modeled black leather miniskirt. "I'll fill you in on the more important details later, Carola."

"Any reason to think he needs respiratory precautions?" Montana asked. The major reason for such precautions would be tuberculosis, a disease Epps was unlikely to have. If he did have TB, they would need to evaluate the people with whom he had been in contact during his hospitalization and at home to see if any of them had become infected. Bella had thought about TB, but not for very long since Belkins' note had indicated he had considered the diagnosis, but that it was so unlikely, no TB tests were needed.

They always finished with a short status report on AIDS. Acquired Immune Deficiency Syndrome had been a constant theme during the past five years. Anxiety within the hospital had waxed and waned, but since the disease and the medical community's understanding of it was evolving so rapidly, the team constantly reevaluated the situation. AIDS was especially time-consuming since there was so much interest, fantasy, and phobia from both the medical staff and the general community.

The end of their conference was like the breaking of a dam. Their secretary had intercepted twenty-three calls and they scrambled to sort them and answer the urgent ones. Bella and Carola set off for the hospital. Montana watched them through the window as they moved down the street, heads bent together under an umbrella, deep in conversation. Montana doubted the walk was long enough to cover the essentials about both Asker and Epps.

MONTANA WORKED for the rest of the afternoon on the Unit's annual report. It was only five months late and so there wasn't any emergency, but Montana never knew when someone from Quality Assurance or Risk Management would call looking for it. When he looked up, it was 5:15. His wife, Molly, a hematologist, was already out rowing on the Schuylkill. She was breaking in her new VanDeusen racing shell, which she had dubbed *Thalassemia,* an allusion both to the sea and to an hereditary blood disorder. If anyone called, her secretary could say she was out working on thalassemia. Montana had to pick up Isaac and Abe at day care in the next fifteen minutes or they would be left out on the steps. Day care was tyranny, unless Montana or Molly needed an excuse to leave a late-afternoon meeting. And poor Jake had been home alone since three o'clock. At twelve, he was a veteran latchkey kid, but three hours alone violated the Montana sense of fair play. And supper wasn't going to reheat itself. The real dilemma was that the day-care center was a ten-minute walk or a twenty-minute drive, given rush-hour traffic in central city. But if he walked there, he and the kids would have to walk back to the car. That walk was at least thirty minutes for a two-year-old and a four-year-old. Hoping against hope, Montana headed for the car.

As usual, the kids received him exuberantly. They babbled away while he paid the late pick-up fine and they maintained a steady stream of enthusiastic and completely unintelligible chatter on the way home. Entry into the Montana home was a carnival. Whimsy doing cartwheels, the little kids chortling, Jake practicing the clarinet, and the TV blaring. Montana loved it, sort of. He changed Abe's diaper, got yesterday's leftover turkey in gear, looked in on Jake, found a cartoon on TV for the kids, and took Whimsy out for his walk.

Molly strode in as they were sitting down to supper. More cartwheels from Whimsy, more chortling from the kids. "Why aren't these kids crying?" she asked as she shed her anorak and shook out her shoulder-length red hair, which hung in moist ringlets. She rubbed three noses and one snout, then sidled up to Montana for a full-throttle thirty-five-second buss. Nobody noticed she was a bit gamy from her workout on the river. Jake, who always finished eating first, sat next to her while she ate and quizzed him about school. He was an active member of the "never tell your parents anything about school" conspiracy. For the four hundredth consecutive day, nothing had happened there. Whimsy parked himself under Abe's chair, which was the area of most frequent food drops, and from whence he could make occasional lunges for other bits that hit the ground. The only problem from Whimsy's point of view was that the food that fell directly on his head tended to stick there and he often ended up wearing Abe's supper instead of eating it.

"What news from you today?" Molly asked Montana as she enticed Abe away from Whimsy's dish and started to put back the noodle-shaped yellow kibble he had picked out from the orange, brown, and red bits. Whimsy stood by, waiting for an opportunity to get his mouth in edgewise.

"The usual. I.D. conference, Human Subjects' meeting, Infection Control meeting. Loren Asker was last night's heart-transplant donor."

"What?"

"Drove his car the wrong way onto the expressway."

"My goodness. Was he the type?"

"I only knew him to nod to. But as far as I know, he wasn't. One of those disgustingly organized, extremely logical guys who keeps a list of everything he does every day."

Molly tsk'd while she helped Isaac open envelopes as they sorted through the pile of mail sitting on the microwave oven. His chubby little fingers carefully extracted a black-bordered announcement from a black-bordered envelope and handed it over. Molly added it to a pile in the back of her recipe file box.

---

### UNIVERSITY OF PENNSYLVANIA

PHILADELPHIA, SEPTEMBER 19

TO MEMBERS OF THE FACULTY AND STAFF:

With great regret I inform you of the death of:

### BENJAMIN ANDREWS CARRUTHERS

PROFESSOR OF MEDICINE, which occurred on the eighth instant, in the fifty-second year of his age.

Your obedient servant,

BAYARD HARPEN
President

---

*19*

"Ben Carruthers. He's the eighth or ninth one this year," she said. "And Asker will be the next. You know, they're all UHOP faculty. You should check it out."

"Check out what, exactly?"

Isaac had gotten to the good stuff, labeled "occupant."

"Check out why your fellow faculty members are dropping like flies, exactly. There's probably some funny business going on."

"They're your fellow faculty members, too. How funny?"

"Funny as in somebody's bumping them off."

"Dearest Molly, I thank the Lord you went into medicine instead of police work. I grant that you were probably correct about Jimmy Hoffa coming to a violent end. Since then you are zero for sixty-seven. Your lifetime of soap operas, detective stories, and gossip columns has warped you beyond the point of no return. People die without any help from guys in trench coats. Even though you're one of the best hematologists in Philadelphia, you bury almost as many patients as you cure."

"Yes, darling, but my patients are all sick and they have a good excuse for dying. These guys are supposed to be iron men and they're sending our group life insurance premiums through the roof." No false modesty, and no yielding on the surmise of foul play.

Montana knew that Molly collected these death notices the way he had once collected baseball cards. Sent by the president of the university, they announced the deaths of full professors, the most senior members of the Penn faculty, in the most formal of terms. She who collected them owned a veritable who's who of modern academic medicine. Her collection, which spanned fifteen years and three presidents, included two Nobel laureates, three Medal of Congress recipients, a bushelful of members of the National Academy of Sciences and the Institute of

**20**

Medicine. The Montanas were untenured, unmedaled, assistant professors; their own passing would go unannounced.

He also knew that she wasn't warped, though her sense of humor was a little twisted. What he really knew, though, was that he'd made a mistake to take the bait at all. If he'd said nothing, she would by now have put away the cards and moved on to politics, or the day-care center's proposal to have parents spend a day a month at the center to improve their "quality time," or a new instructional aid for teaching hematology to medical students.

On the other hand, she had crossed the line from her usual idle speculation ("Somebody's bumping them off") to inference based on real data. Sort of. She was on his turf. Epidemiology used data from many individuals to learn about nature. Although Montana cared for patients one at a time like other physicians, he spent much of his time considering them in the aggregate. One infection rarely told anything about who or how. Two or three raised some possibilities. A few dozen often spoke volumes.

Seeing this as one of those rare opportunities to raise Molly's epidemiologic consciousness, Montana took the plunge. "How many people have died, exactly?" The first thing an epidemiologist needs is an accurate count.

Molly beamed. After all these years, Montana was finally playing the game with her. "Nine so far this year, counting Asker, and I bet there'll be a lot of others."

"Let's not count them just yet. How many were there last year?"

"Six, and six the year before that."

"So, this year is already ahead of them," said Montana. Molly smiled. Isaac was busily drawing smiley faces on the empty envelopes; Molly balanced Abe on her hip and gradually cleared the meal mess.

"Maybe we should draw an epidemic curve," he continued. Laying out the cards on the kitchen table in columns, Montana dealt a macabre game of solitaire. Each column represented a year. The height of the column corresponded to the number of deaths. The column with this year's eight cards (soon to be nine) was noticeably taller than the others. Molly smiled again.

"Now let's sort them into the UHOP group and the other Penn staff." The second thing an epidemiologist needs to do is to classify cases accurately. He separated each column into two. Now he had side-by-side pairs of columns. The left-hand column in each pair had UHOP deaths; the right-hand column had the others. In each of the preceding pairs, the two columns were the same height, with three cards apiece. In this year's pair, the UHOP column towered over the other, totaling seven (soon to be eight) to one. Molly grinned. Isaac made columns of envelopes with windows, envelopes with pictures, and plains.

"Of course, we need a lot of other information. It doesn't make sense to count just the deaths. We have to know how many people there are in the two faculty groups. If the UHOP faculty grew, you'd expect to see more deaths. We'd have to check with the personnel office."

"HUP just added two new pavilions and a 150,000-square-foot research tower. UHOP hasn't changed since it was built." She smiled graciously. Her lab and practice were based at the Hospital of the University of Pennsylvania—HUP, on the Penn campus.

"Or the UHOP group might be a lot older," Montana continued. The third thing an epidemiologist needs to do is to make sure that the groups being compared are truly comparable in all other ways except for the feature being examined (UHOPness). He wanted to be sure she received the full benefit of this tutorial.

"Carruthers was fifty-one. None of the others was

over sixty. Not what you usually think of as the geriatric set." She smiled enigmatically. "This is really much more interesting than blood. And you get to do it all the time. I'm very jealous."

Montana knew enough to accept an honorable disengagement when one was offered. He agreed that epidemiology really was satisfying, once one got the hang of it, and he scooped the cards into a single pile and handed them to Molly, who put them back behind a recipe for ratatouille.

Montana spent the next hour putting the two younger kids to bed. "Daddy, today's the name story," said Isaac.

"No, it isn't. The name story is on Wednesday. Tonight's the story about how I fished Mommy out of the river when her boat tipped over."

"No, no, that story's on Monday. Today *is* Wednesday."

"It is? Are you sure? I know yesterday was Tuesday. Doesn't Monday come after Tuesday?"

"No. Daddy, it's very important to learn that."

Abe, who'd been waiting for his cue, chimed in, "Monday, Tuesday, Wednesday . . ."

"Okay, okay, if you're both sure it's Wednesday, here goes." Victorious, they settled in for the story, ready to pounce if Montana omitted a detail. "Once upon a time, there was a doctor named Dr. Archer. He cured lots of people and became very famous. He had a little girl who grew up and got married and had a little boy, who grew up, and so on and so forth. All of the little boys and girls grew up and had other boys and girls until one of them had a little girl who was . . ."

"Grandma!" they shouted in unison.

"Right. Keep that in mind. Now there was another doctor, named Dr. Rush. He also cured lots of people and became very famous. He had a little boy who grew up and got married and had a little girl, who grew up, and so on and so forth, and all of the little girls and boys grew up and had other boys and girls until one of them had a little . . ."

"Puppy!"

"Very funny. But I'm the one who tells the jokes in this story. Well, it so happens it was Grandpa. And when Grandpa and Grandma had me, they decided it would be nice if I was named for their great-great-great-great-great-great-great-grandpas, so they named me Archer Rush. Only, people used to say to them, 'Your boy has three last names.' They said, 'That's okay, because we call him Monty, so his real last name acts like a first name.' So everybody called me Monty, except my grandma, who called me 'Sagittarius.' And that, best beloved, is how Archer Rush Montana got his names."

They didn't understand the classical reference but insisted on it nonetheless. They allowed Montana to tuck them in, the Isaac murmured, "Maybe it is Monday." Abe giggled. Montana groaned theatrically and left.

Montana spent the rest of the evening working on the Epidemiology Unit's report. By the time he finished, he found Molly in bed herself, watching "Dynasty" with the headphones on. Whimsy lay next to her. Montana pushed the dog toward the foot of the bed, extracted an edge of blanket from under him, and slid into bed, the dog's chin resting on his knee.

Montana read while Molly watched TV. Suddenly he felt her hand on his arm.

"Vanning Epps was hospitalized at UHOP," she said in the too-loud tone of a headset wearer.

"I know. He has some two-bit pneumonia and Dan Belkins brought him in for a rest." He replied loudly so she could hear.

"No, it isn't. I'm *sure* it isn't. Remember when we saw him at the opera last month. I told you he'd lost weight and was breathing fast. And how his hair was dull and his skin was shiny. He looked terrible. I thought it was arsenic."

"He looked okay to me. And arsenic turns your skin dark and scaly, not shiny."

"Whatever. I bet it's part of whatever's going on with the UHOP faculty."

"Wait a second. First of all, he's not dying, and second, he's not on the faculty."

"He's honorary. I'm sure I'll get his card when the time comes."

"He certainly isn't based at UHOP."

"Yeah, but most of his donations go there. You should be a little less picky about small details." The news faded and she turned off the light.

Montana wasn't going to win this debate and he wasn't about to lose a second one in a single evening. He cast about for a diversion. Whimsy came to the rescue, letting out a quiet growl as he began to dream.

"Come here, big fella," Molly called softly in the dark.

"Are you talking to the dog?"

"Nope."

## FOUR

NEITHER OF them could sleep, and it was still raining at midnight when Montana and Whimsy made their way back to the kitchen. Montana spent two hours shuffling

25

the black-edged cards, but the UHOP group still towered over the others. There were statistical tests for deciding the probability of having a split as uneven as this one, but he would need more details on the dead men and their still-quick colleagues. The question was whether to make the effort to get them. Even with approximate numbers, he could tell that Molly was right and the excess was highly improbable.

On the other hand, one of the few things that years of epidemiology had taught him was that improbability was very common. Life was full of coincidences. College roommates with the same birthday. Larry Bird going ten for ten in the fourth quarter of a play-off game. Lightning striking twice in the same place. But there were lots of dorms, many, many basketball games, and a lot of places where thunderstorms occur. The chances that the same dorm room would have matching roommates next year, or that Larry would be hot the next quarter, or that the eighteenth tee would be hit during the next storm were pretty remote. UHOP's obituaries were interesting but almost certainly a coincidence.

On yet the final hand, much of what Montana did was to investigate clusters of three or four infections to find out whether they were coincidences or not. The trick was to decide which ones to pursue. The improbability of an epidemic of deaths among the senior faculty was counter-balanced by its importance if it was genuine. Especially since he and Molly might someday be senior faculty. Seen in that light, it was worth a bit more time.

By dawn, he had outlined an approach. He and Whimsy toured the neighborhood, taking longer than usual because it was trash pick-up day and the streets were an olfactory gold mine. They returned to find Molly breakfasting on coffee and butterscotch Tastycakes. During the half hour before the kids woke, he laid out the plan.

**26**

"You mean you're really going to work this up?" Molly asked incredulously.

"You said we should look into it. I'm taking you at your word. Here's how we should divide it up."

"Actually, I said you should look into it. Am I going to have to learn the Hansel and Gretel equation?"

"You mean Mantel–Haenszel, and the answer's no. We need to use shoe leather, not fancy math. You find out all of the Penn medical faculty who've died in the last year. We only get notices for the senior staff. We need to know if this involves junior faculty, too."

"More bodies. Sounds like fun. What are you going to do?"

"You're not finished. While you're talking to the people at Penn, find out how many full-time faculty positions there are."

"Right. So, what are you going to do?"

"I'll do Temple and Jeff. We also need to know if this is restricted to Penn."

"I'll phone them. If you don't mind. Maybe they'll put me on their mailing list." She realized there might be a whole world of different series of death announcements.

"Okay, I'll get the death certificates, medical examiner's reports, and anything else there is about the causes of death."

"I want to do that part, too. Is there anything else you can do?"

"I'll work on the causal chain."

"I wish you'd stop talking like a seventeenth-century philosopher and just say you'll dream up some way that a bunch of guys should die prematurely. How are you going to do that?"

"The usual way. I'll see if they had anything special to do with each other at UHOP. And maybe if they had any relationships with each other outside the hospital. And just talk to people who worked with them to see if I get any more ideas."

"Maybe we should work on that part together. What about the guys in the trench coats?"

"We aren't going to look for trench coats, unless you want to buy one. Remember, most of these men died of natural causes. Even if there's something to this business, it isn't somebody switching signs on the expressway ramps."

"Hmm. Don't forget to include Epps in your casual chain."

"Epps isn't dead."

Molly opened her mouth but the conversation went no further, because children appeared in various states of undress, demanding attention and breakfast.

MONTANA SAW a TV van with its microwave antenna extended parked outside the hospital's main entrance. Epps. When the emperor caught a cold, lots of people sneezed. After rounding with the still-smiling intern who had presented the case at yesterday's conference, Montana went up to the gold coast to look at Epps's chart.

It was important, in any event, to exclude the possibility that Epps had something infectious that would require respiratory isolation. Because of the man's celebrity status, everyone was being even more thorough than usual. TB, unlikely as it was, given the history Bella had gleaned from the chart, was the only disease to worry about in this setting. Epps was old enough to have been infected during childhood and to have had a dormant infection since then. Most TB in adults is a reactivation of such an infection. Fifty years ago, TB had been one of the most common problems in the hospital, but now it was relatively rare, occurring principally in the elderly, in immigrants from underdeveloped countries, the poor, and, increasingly, in AIDS patients. Still, it did occur from time to time in all sorts of people, and the admonition always to consider TB had been a standard part of the medical school curriculum since the turn of the century when it was known at the "white plague." Good physicians usually considered the diagnosis, as Belkins had. The problem, as in much of medicine, was to decide when to press on to make the diagnosis, when the initial evidence was against it. Good physicians had certainly mistakenly discounted TB, an error that could have lethal implications, as Eleanor Roosevelt's physicians discovered.

For the first time Montana could remember, the medical chart wasn't lying around where any passerby in a white coat could read it. An executive assistant who clearly didn't work for the hospital established Montana's reason for wanting the chart, checked his credentials, and retrieved the loose-leaf binder from Epps's room. As Montana expected, Bella had summarized all of the useful information. Simple pneumonia, unresponsive to a couple of days' antibiotics at home. Some weight loss and fatigue. Not much help in deciding for or against TB.

His next stop was the X-ray department to have a look at Epps's chest film. He always found the X-ray reading room a soothing oasis. It took about a minute to adjust from the harsh glare of fluorescents on stainless to the subdued glow of indirects on wood paneling and soft brown pile carpeting. Around the room were seven garage-door-sized banks of view boxes that could hold a hundred films and backlight ten at a time. Only one was lit now, as the solitary radiology resident examined new films from the emergency room. Montana waved to the woman, who smiled without interrupting her dictation. He punched Epps's hospital number into a terminal, and suddenly one of the machines rumbled to life, fishing a row of Epps's films from its innards. Montana walked over to it as the lights turned on, illuminating six ghostlike images of Epps's chest. He settled into an orthopedically designed swivel chair that exacerbated his underlying jealousy of radiologists and inspected the films.

His look didn't really help. The X ray was clearly abnormal, but there were none of the classic signs of TB. No old scars in the lungs, no calcified lymph nodes, no well-defined areas of pneumonia. Just a diffuse hazy shadow in several areas. The film didn't point to a diagnosis of TB, but it didn't rule it out, either. It was still most likely a common simple viral infection that would heal on its own.

Montana made a note to talk to Belkins about getting Epps's sputum examined for TB. A diligent search through the microscope by an experienced observer sometimes revealed the tubercle bacilli themselves, also known as "red snappers" because of their characteristic color when stained with a combination of dyes. Easiest, perhaps, to offer to do the stain and exam himself, since Belkins might be justifiably sensitive about having the question of TB raised in a way that every lab technician and the TV van at the front door would soon know about. He spun himself around a couple of times in the wonderful swivel chair before starting off for his first meeting of the day, the Executive Committee.

*SIX*

THE EXECUTIVE Committee, or EC (pronounced "eck"), set medical policy for UHOP. Composed of the chiefs of the clinical departments plus a few hangers-on, it ordinarily approved decisions forwarded to it by other committees, which approved decisions forwarded to them by. . . . This meeting, however, promised something different. The topic was AIDS and the EC was ad-libbing. That is, it didn't know before it started what it was going to decide—or what its chairman and hospital president, Robert Perrin Larraby, M.D., M.A, (Oxon), D.Sc. (Hon.), wanted it to decide. Montana attended a couple of these meetings each year, always at the request of Larraby's office, when the committee discussed a topic related to Hospital Epidemiology. Half of those times, he was ignored. For the rest, he was asked to discuss some event or policy that a department chairman didn't like. All things considered, he'd rather be in Philadelphia.

Larraby convened the meeting with many pleasantries. It was part of the style that distinguished him from his counterparts at other hospitals. He was arguably one of the brightest physicians in the country. He had conducted seminal research on vesicles and had embarked on an extraordinary scientific career before becoming president of the hospital ten years earlier. He had proven to be a remarkable administrator as well, conceiving of the idea of the hybrid hospital and convincing the three medical schools to work together to charter a jointly owned and staffed institution. This had been widely believed to be an impossible feat, because Jefferson had been suspicious of Penn since the 1820s when Penn had petitioned the state legislature to close the upstart new school. And both institutions had only marginal respect for Temple, which they believed had never truly outgrown its origin as a turn-of-the-century evening medical school. Larraby had orchestrated the merger of the three hospitals, each of which thought the sun rose and set on itself. He single-handedly moved the plans for this new building past hundreds of internal committees and myriad local, state, and national regulatory bodies. He attracted physicians and researchers of international stature to the institution. Larraby himself achieved national standing because of these successes.

"All of us have spent more time dealing with the AIDS problem than we'd like. Several of you have raised the need for new policies. I've set aside today's meeting so we can clear the air and get on with the real business of running this hospital. Dr. Nivel, why don't you begin?"

Montana pondered Larraby's statement. There was every reason to believe that AIDS would become the real business of the hospital. UHOP's intensive care beds weren't completely filled with AIDS patients, as was the case in some hospitals in New York and San Francisco. But if the predictions were remotely true, in five years there would be ten times as many cases as there were now, and UHOP would be living and breathing AIDS. And even the half dozen patients on UHOP's wards now strained the hospital's resources. Just about everyone with AIDS eventually died from it. And how they died—demented, or with purple skin cancers, or unable to breathe. Things were only a little better since AZT, a chemical discovered in herring sperm, was shown to keep

**32**

a lid on the disease. AZT was no longer tough to get, but it had lots of complications of its own, in addition to bankrupting the patients who needed thousands of dollars a year to pay for it. Beyond their formidable medical problems, AIDS patients were frequently cut loose from society. They were often too sick to work, or they were forced out of their jobs. Many were unable to live at home, or their homes wouldn't have them back. Some couldn't bear to tell their families what they had, or their families wouldn't hear it. And that was for the first wave of AIDS patients, mostly white, middle-class gays, with jobs and families and lots of places to turn for support. The second wave, IV drug users who started with none of these, were even worse off. And the cases that would be coming soon, wives and partners and children of these patients, would tax the staff and the support network in ways no one could imagine. No surprise then that a black cloud hung over the wards that cared for patients with AIDS. Barring a miracle, AIDS surely would be the business of the hospital for many years to come. But that wasn't the subject of this EC discussion, as Nivel was pointing out.

"Didn't think I'd live to see the day, but for the first time in twenty-five years, the surgical staff is talking about something beside malpractice and/or reimbursement." Sam Nivel's fortyish years as a department chairmen and trainer of a generation of other department chairmen had given him a long fuse. Or vice versa. A fair-haired boy when he took over the department in 1948, he now had a pate that glistened in the glare of the recessed spotlights dotting the ceiling. Nivel hadn't lived in Texas for at least fifty years, but you couldn't tell that from his twang. "Some young fellas in my department"— by this he meant anyone under sixty-five—"think cutting on people with AIDS is too risky. They take a dim view of catching it, which they figure will happen if they poke themselves in the finger while they're operating on an infected patient. 'How risky can it be,' I asked 'em, 'when it hasn't happened after all this time?' They say maybe it hasn't and maybe it has, depending on what you believe about that guy in Cleveland, who some say had a lot of other risky behavior and some say he didn't. They say, in any event, they don't plan on being the first case."

"Physicians are obliged to provide care, their own danger not withstanding," said L. Terrence Smythe, the Chief of Medicine, who had been Larry Smith until college and had acquired an accent to match his new name during a sabbatical at Oxford. He could always be counted on for a supercilious remark. "My department has never shirked its responsibilities for those patients. My dear Nivel, you must be able to make them acknowledge their obligations."

Nivel had long since stopped taking offense. "Could be your 'department' might feel different if it was standing for hours up to its elbows in somebody's infected blood instead of putting a stethoscope on his chest. Anyway they aren't saying any of that stuff; I'm interpreting for them. What they say is, first of all, people with AIDS, or even folks who don't have AIDS but who got that virus that causes it, don't heal up well after surgery, so you shouldn't be so quick to operate on 'em. Now they don't really know how those poor bastards heal up, but they've convinced themselves it's true, so they're still 'acknowledging their obligations' like you say, L.T. They also say, if they are going to do those operations, they need to know who's infected and who isn't so they can use the right technique. So they want to test everybody before they operate on 'em."

A nameless corporate lawyer signaled for Larraby's attention. "As I'm sure you know, Dr. Nivel, state law strictly forbids mandatory serologic testing of patients. Even voluntary testing requires counseling."

"Well, of course it does, Sonny. But there hasn't been

a law yet that can't be changed. The local surgical society has fifteen state legislators cosponsoring a bill to require everybody to get tested. The U.S. Centers for Disease Control isn't going to stand in the way and neither is the Supreme Court. So I expect it'll be legal real soon."

True enough, thought Montana. The CDC had been a bastion of reason and a reliable resource upon which one could depend for factual authoritative support in discussions with the zealots, reactionaries, and just plain fearful folks who wanted to keep infected kids out of school, quarantine carriers, and generally disenfranchise those who were infected with HIV, the Human Immunodeficiency Virus—the cause of AIDS. But that was before the outfit got its marching orders from Washington. The new CDC line was a mass of vague advice that let any state, municipality, or hospital justify mandatory screening of anybody for just about any reason. Montana remembered the old lawyer's saying, "When the facts are on your side, pound the facts. When the law's on your side, pound the law. When neither's on your side, pound the table." With the CDC's capitulation in the public-policy arena, it was time to pound the law. But pretty soon the legislature would make it table-pounding time.

"How come none of you sharpies wants to know how they're gonna change their technique when they know their patient's infected?" Nivel was still talking. "They're going to use *good* technique. No holding the needle with their fingers. No sewing where they can't see, so they have to use their fingers to figure out where the end of the needle is, just like you do when you diaper a baby. Now, I'm telling you there isn't a man or woman among them that shouldn't be doing that all the time, no matter if the patient has hemophilia or is some little old lady from the Old Sod Nursing Home. It's no wonder they get more hepatitis than you can shake a stick at.

"So here's what UHOP oughtta do. Tell those scalpel

jockeys they better use their best behavior for everybody, or they can't operate at all. And that they can't test their patients just because they're planning to operate. I'd do both those things myself if I could, but I can't stop them from ordering tests, and I want to make sure you wise men and women will back me on the operating-room procedure business. I don't mind taking a stand, I just don't fancy doing it on a cloud."

Larraby scanned the group, looking for comment. Seeing none, he raised an eyebrow in Montana's direction. Montana cleared his throat.

"It's important to remember that it's extremely difficult to acquire HIV infection in the hospital, or anywhere else, unless you have intercourse"—this roomful of physicians averted its gaze and shifted in its chairs—"with an infected person or get a sizable exposure to the person's blood. The risk of infection is about a half percent after a bloody needlestick from an infected person. And there was that famous announcement in 1987 about three people who got infected after blood splashed on a cut or in their eyes or mouths. So it's pretty clear that even minor exposures *can* transmit HIV, even if the chance is one in a million. Even though it's a very rare event, the fact of the matter is that everybody who works in the hospital has gotten splashed hundreds of times, so everybody's uneasy. If you're infected with HIV, you have a pretty good chance of getting AIDS eventually.

"As I look at it, there are only two ways to go, universal testing or universal precautions. One is to figure out who all the infected people are; the other is to treat all patients as though they are infected, the way Dr. Nivel proposes. We've been advocating just such a form of universal precautions for some time. It turns out that universal precautions mostly really means doing things that were a good idea before any of us ever heard of AIDS. Like wearing gloves to change an IV or to empty a bedpan. And disinfecting instruments before reusing them. If we're consistent about those things, we'll have a higher level of protection than we would if we wore space suits to take care of the people we know are infected, and we won't have to worry about testing, or notifying, or maintaining confidentiality of the HIV-antibody test results.

"I don't see an advantage to universal testing unless we could satisfy ourselves there are some sensible precautions that can't be applied universally. I don't know of any in the labs, but there conceivably could be in the OR. If it really proves safer for the surgeon to make bigger incisions, for instance, we'd have to think twice about subjecting all of the patients to extra-long scars and the longer anesthesia time. Or if inexperienced surgeons are much more likely to cut themselves, we might not want them to operate on infected patients. I don't know of any solid evidence for any of these things, but they are worth exploring. Until we get some evidence, I think universal precautions are best, as Dr. Nivel suggests."

Now there were plenty of people with comments. The Vice-President for Garbage stroked his waxed mustache and said, "If you do away with special precautions for patients with AIDS, this place will make the 1986 garbage strike look like Neatness Day at *Better Homes and Gardens,* because there isn't a dump in the state that'll take our trash. And if you put everybody on AIDS precautions, our hazardous-waste-disposal bill will be more than Frank Rizzo ever dreamed of pocketing. Either way, we'll be ruined."

Montana was ready. "Bella's spoken to the Department of Public Health about the idea of universal precautions. They're at peace with the idea as long as the really bloody stuff is handled separately, just the way it is now."

Daren Ang, Chief of Pathology and Vice-President for Clinical Laboratories, a man of indeterminate age and national origin, withdrew from his briefcase a half-inch-thick sheaf of papers and brandished it at Montana. "Doctor, my staff knows of your plans and will not tolerate them. These are letters of resignation from sixty laboratory technicians who will leave this institution if you stop identifying samples from patients with AIDS. They have contacted their union, and the state labor board has begun an inquiry into your planned relaxation of safety standards. I cannot acquiesce to your proposal."

Montana realized the man was in a difficult position— whether he personally believed labeling was a good idea or not. Montana gave it his best shot. "Professor Ang, your laboratory's own guidelines say explicitly that all samples should be handled as though they are infectious. If that's the case, I don't see how it helps to have some of the infected samples marked as such. We all know that only about half of the ones we know are infected are ever labeled. And none of the ones we don't know about are labeled. Besides, the American Hospital Association, OSHA, and the Centers for Disease Control said they saw no advantage to marking infectious samples."

As Montana talked, Ang shuffled the letters he was holding. He began to read the letters he was holding, when Larraby intervened.

"We'll have to wait on that, Professor Ang. And I'm afraid we won't be able to hear from the nursing side, either." This was in deference to the Vice-President for Nursing, a littermate of Carrie Nation's, who had been waving her pencil in the air for some time. "I see that this issue will need a bit more discussion. Dr. Smythe, will you form a working group to develop recommendations for this committee? Dr. Montana's points are important ones, but I trust your group will take into account the concerns of all parties. Please keep in mind that we have an obligation to maintain the functional integrity of this institution. It won't do to be right and to have our surgeons operating at the Bryn Mawr Hospital, or for our trash bill to go through the roof. I'll expect you to report to us in a month. Meanwhile, I know you'll continue to make a good-faith effort to keep your respective staffs happy. Dr. Montana, that will mean having your staff notify relevant personnel of all infected patients."

Larraby closed the meeting with his most conciliatory smile and left the committee to disband in evil humor.

## SEVEN

MOLLY HAD had a long day. "Did you know that personnel officers won't talk to you on the phone? And if you go there, they won't tell you who or how old or even what your own salary is? We'd need a court order to get that information out of them. I shifted to plan B."

Montana watched as she extracted from her duffel bag six half-inch-thick telephone directories—one from each school for the past two academic years. "Ahh, plan B." Montana appreciated improvisation.

"Everybody who died is in one of last year's books, and absent from this year's, the most recently deceased excepted. If you will turn to the Senior Faculty section of last year's books and read the names aloud, I'll check them against this year's books. When you read a name I can't find, I'll let you know and you can mark the name in your book."

"Of course, most people who leave don't die. Offers for bigger labs, division-head jobs, lucrative practices, tenure decisions gone awry, turf battles lost, grants not renewed. That's perfectly all right for a start. It will let us winnow down the possibilities to a list we can investigate."

It took them four hours to wade through the three pairs of books. There were checks next to three hundred names that had disappeared. Included among these were the original eight who had piqued Molly's interest. Between them, they knew 258 who had simply left, and two more who had died. One was a radiologist from Temple who had appeared on lots of local talk shows advocating annual ultrasound examinations of the prostate as the male equivalent of breast-cancer screening. The other was a professor of psychiatry from Jefferson who had been electrocuted while administering electroconvulsive therapy in the Depressive Disorders Clinic.

"So?" asked Molly.

"So, you're at least partly right."

"Told you."

"We still have to check the other forty missing names, but both of these additional deaths were at UHOP and there aren't any deaths we know of yet at the other hospitals. We can't say much either way about whether the faculty at UHOP has more than its fair share. You'd expect more Penn deaths since its faculty is bigger than the other two schools."

"We can guesstimate the size of the faculties at the different places," she said. "There are thirty pages of names in the Penn directory and ten pages in each of the other two. There are about forty names per page. It looks as though about half in each book had a UHOP address, but I'll do an exact count tomorrow."

"And I'll get my secretary to call their telephone numbers in the old book and see if they answer. I'll tell her I need to update their addresses for a mailing. Then it's back to the casual chain."

"We already know how everybody died. That's common knowledge." She pulled out the cards and started to enumerate the causes of death. "Asker died in that crash; Carruthers had a stroke; Roy Davis—MI; Mario Garelli—hypercalcemia. Boy, that was weird. I'd never heard of a real-life milk-alkali syndrome before that one."

Montana agreed. Every medical student knew that the combination of large amounts of milk plus calcium containing antacids, such as TUMS or Rolaids, could, in principle, raise the concentration of calcium in the blood to dangerous levels. The condition was seen rarely before modern prescription antacids came to be standard therapy for ulcers, and it was almost unheard of these days. Garelli, a molecular biologist, had treated his own indigestion for weeks with increasing doses of antacid, without ever getting a practicing internist to advise him. The first anyone knew of the problem, he was admitted with renal failure and died soon thereafter from multiple complications.

Molly plowed on. "Harold Levy had an MI."

"What's an MI?" Jake had sauntered into the kitchen, looking for a Ring Ding. He was carrying the draft of a letter he'd written to William Safire, asking whether when he had blackened his mother's eye with a badly pitched baseball, he had committed child abuse, and, if so, was he a child abuser.

"Myocardial infarction, dear. It's the technical term for a heart attack." She went on through the cards. "Sandor Loaming succumbed after all those years to alcoholic hepatitis. Charlotte North drowned on vacation in Bimini. Simon Thompson had an MI. That leaves Jordan Wicks, who died of peritonitis after his ulcerative colitis flared and he developed toxic megacolon."

"Plus those two new ones," Montana added. "Orenberg the shrink and Mustafa Rus the radiologist with the brain tumor."

"I don't see how those could have anything to do with one another," Molly said. "And none of them looks like murder," she said sadly. "Maybe only some of them fit."

"Murder never seemed a reasonable bet," Montana said. "And you're probably right that they might not all be related. We won't know unless we figure out the pattern."

"You mean like seeing if they were in the same army unit in Vietnam, or if they all lived in the same neighborhood or had the same secretary with a tight dress?"

"Anything you can put together. Let's get their CVs tomorrow."

"What's a CV?" Jake had taken a seat.

"A list of professional accomplishments. It's short for curriculum vitae. It tells what schools you went to, what jobs you had, and what articles you've written. It's also got some stuff about where you were born and how many kids you have."

"Do you and Mom have one?"

"Sure."

"Can I see them?"

"Sure, why?"

"I want to see us on them."

"Will do." Montana made a note to add the kids' names and ages to his CV before bringing it home.

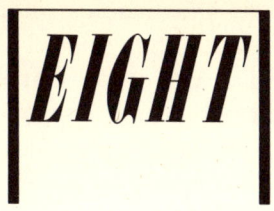

# EIGHT

THE EPIDEMIOLOGY team spent nearly all of the next day's meeting on implementation of the new AIDS policies, especially as they affected notification of hospital workers. Carola was particularly effective at translating abstract policies into the way people work every day—intuitive, sensitive, and practical. It was also the way she organized her life—a professional cellist with a regular paycheck from the hospital. Nights and weekends with the Curtis String Quartet, days with Hospital Epidemiology. Comfortable and challenged in both worlds, with a chameleon's ability to change her image. The Salvation Army on Market Street was her clothier and she looked fabulous in anything. These days, she sported various ensembles of Brooks Brothers teen clothes. In an effort to maintain some semblance of confidentiality, Carola had convinced the lab directors to accept a statement that the "special precautions" list would not just be for AIDS but also for people who had or might have other serious blood-borne diseases, such as hepatitis B or Creutzfeldt-Jakob disease. Part of the system already worked well. It was possible to notify the administrator of lab control of new precaution patients and to see the list appear in each of the twenty-two laboratories within a day. Not so good was that each lab insisted on posting the list on the wall for every passerby to see, or that all the old lists stayed up, with a cross next to the names of patients who had died. The whole system was running on xeroxed pieces of paper that floated around.

They previewed a videotape Carola and Bella were making for hospital personnel. It provided general information on AIDS, discussed the new policies, and reviewed the essentials of good hygiene. It was a great film, with plenty of information and campy entertainment value. Shot on location, without professional lighting, makeup, or a gyrocam, the tape literally jumped from scene to scene and included occasional shots of ceilings, floors, and empty corridors. It ended with a semiprofessional fade to darkness punctuated by giggling on the still-active sound track.

They also reviewed a variety of "improved" methods that had sprung up for cleaning and disinfecting items that had come into contact with blood or other effluvia from AIDS patients. The proper procedures were clear and direct and had been performed on *all* equipment without incident for the past several years by the staff in central processing. Now, as a result of the new policies that called for CPD to be notified when specific pieces of equipment had been used for an AIDS patient, CPD had spontaneously added a bewildering array of individual extra practices "for insurance." Bella reported the demise of a five-thousand-dollar bronchoscope, a marvel of lenses and lights that could be threaded through the mouth into the lungs in order to inspect the airways or to snip out samples of lung tissue to use for various kinds of tests. Yesterday, one had been used for an AIDS patient, and a well-meaning and unfortunately creative CPD technician immersed the whole thing in iodine for twenty minutes before carrying on with the usual disinfection. This added precaution had the unanticipated effect of rendering the optical system completely and permanently opaque.

*44*

"The people in CPD insist someone told them to do it that way. I left it at that and was trying to find a departmental budget to purchase a replacement when a cloud with a silver lining sailed by. It turns out Dr. Belkins isn't satisfied with the progress of Mr. Epps's pneumonia, and he wants to bronch him this afternoon. At the moment, there isn't a functioning scope in the building, so Epps's secretary ordered one and had his jet pick it up this morning from the factory. Epps is going to donate it to the hospital."

It was a sign of the times that a hospital with a $700 million annual budget couldn't cover an unanticipated five-thousand-dollar expense without major heartache. It was good news, in a way, that it didn't need to this time. It was bad news, though, that Epps needed bronchoscopy. It was beginning to sound as though this was not a simple garden-variety pneumonia. Maybe he had choked on a chicken bone (well, perhaps a pheasant bone). From an Epidemiology perspective, it still wasn't a problem. Epps's failure to improve kept the possibility of TB alive, however. Montana doubted the chest X ray could have changed enough to warrant another look, but he kept the problem on his worry list, well below the string of deaths he and Molly were pursuing. Epps's well-being aside, Montana knew the press would have a field day with the possibility that Epps had TB. Montana didn't look forward to having to trace the man's contacts while an army of reporters followed him.

On his way home, he picked up the "mailing list" his secretary had prepared of the forty unaccounted for academics from last year's telephone books. All of them had moved on to earthly rewards. He also retrieved the CVs from the medical library. The men and woman who had died had been successful academics, no doubt about it. On average, they had published 150 articles apiece and had served on a slew of national commissions. The cream of the crop. And not a hint of a common thread.

# NINE

THE NEXT morning Montana stopped at the pathology laboratory to see whether they had any results yet from Epps's bronchoscopy. He found Ang, who was an accomplished pulmonary pathologist in addition to being a cantankerous administrator, and Dan Belkins sitting knee to knee at a two-headed microscope. Belkins yielded his spot to Montana.

"This is incredible. The lung is full of owls' eyes. Monty, Epps has CMV pneumonia."

Montana was almost totally ignorant when it came to diagnosing pathology specimens through the microscope. But even he appreciated the distorted morphology of those lung cells that seemed to be looking back up at him through the scope. Ang was certain—this was cytomegalovirus, or CMV, pneumonia. It is one of the few causes of pneumonia that could be diagnosed by eye. They surveyed a number of other areas on the slide, with Montana and Belkins taking turns. Every field of view showed the same thing, a far-advanced case of cytomegalovirus pneumonia.

This was wholly unexpected. Cytomegalovirus is a virus that made peace with the human species long ago. Many children pick it up, often from other children, especially in places such as day-care centers, where saliva and urine are much in evidence. It might give them a little fever for a few days, but they invariably recover without benefit of medical diagnosis or intervention. But, like TB, it persists in the body forever. Unlike TB, it is almost never heard from again.

CMV pneumonia like this was usually a consequence of high-tech medical care. By and large, the only adults who developed serious infections had a correspondingly serious disturbance of their bodies' defense mechanisms. In order to transplant organs or to treat many forms of cancer, it was necessary to suppress host defenses. This suppression also allowed microbes such as CMV, which had been held in check for many years, to cause illness.

But Epps didn't have cancer or a transplanted kidney. Until twenty minutes ago, he had been a healthy guy with a cough who was taking it easy in the hospital. Now he was a patient who was going to have to fight for his life. Montana asked Belkins whether Epps had received any drugs or radiation treatments that might have allowed this infection to erupt.

"Nothing, Monty. The man's been healthy as an ox since I started caring for him ten years ago. The only other time he was hospitalized was last year, when he had hip surgery. I hospitalized him now because he had trouble shaking this cough and he was getting ready for a lot of important meetings. I convinced him that he could rest better here. He has no more right to this infection than you or I."

"Right or not, he has it. If he isn't getting any medical therapy that's put him in line for it, you better figure out what else is wrong with him. Dan, could he have AIDS?"

"Of course not; he's a real straight arrow and monogamous as the day is long. The only drug that guy ever took without a physician's advice was aspirin."

"But you realize that unless you find some other explanation, he has AIDS by definition. He has a clear-cut opportunistic infection without any predisposing cause. If it is AIDS, his HIV-antibody test is probably positive. But CMV pneumonia in this guy makes it the best bet."

Even the possibility that Epps could have AIDS sank in slowly. If it was true, Epps was doomed. Even if he survived this infection, he would almost surely succumb to some other complication of the disease. AZT might buy him time, but it wouldn't cure him. Beyond that, the social implications of his having AIDS would be enormous. Almost every sentient being in the United States over age twelve knew who was at risk for getting AIDS. And everyone knew Epps didn't have hemophilia.

Other public figures had had AIDS. Rock Hudson's illness had propelled the disease into the public view and almost single-handedly provoked a new level of hysteria. But Epps was different. He was no social butterfly. He was a pillar of society and an important example of individual commitment to positive social values, both on a national and international level. His having AIDS would not cause as much turmoil as it would in the President or the Pope, but it would be close.

Montana interrupted this line of thought, mostly because he was having a hard time imagining that Epps was gay. Despite years of revelations about skeletons in famous closets, this image simply didn't fit Epps. Montana and Belkins started talking at the same time. Montana stopped because he didn't like what he was going to say.

"Monty, I guess you're technically correct that he meets the case definition for AIDS, but it just doesn't make sense. And you know that there might be other explanations for this pneumonia. I don't think we have enough yet to call it AIDS. I'll talk to him about getting some other studies."

This suited Montana. Caution in accepting this diagnosis made sense medically as well as psychologically; it was the best way to avoid missing something else. It also spared Epps the possibility of being given a death sentence incorrectly. If he really had AIDS, he'd know it soon enough.

"Dan, we have another problem, too. Whether Epps has AIDS or not, the chance is high enough that we need to change his isolation precautions. The idiotic new policy of giving patients' names to the labs means the newspapers are a cinch to hear about it within seconds. And I guarantee you they won't trouble themselves with the subtleties of the situation."

Belkins started to explain to Montana why this notification policy was completely illogical. Montana cut him short.

"The question isn't whether the rule makes sense or whether it makes people safer; the only issue I can see is how to avoid having it blow up in our faces. It's Larraby's rule; he needs to deal with it. If you want, I'll work on that part while you see Epps."

Montana found a private phone in one of the autopsy rooms and called Larraby's office. Larraby was in Washington, chairing a meeting of the Council on Health Policy, a presidential advisory committee. With some difficulty, Montana extracted the telephone number in Washington from Larraby's secretary, called the Department of Health and Human Services, which was the Council's sponsor, and left word for Larraby to call as soon as possible. He ran to his office, hoping the page wouldn't come through before he got there.

Out of breath and thankful that his beeper hadn't gone off, Montana logged on to the computer and immediately selected "HUNT," the hospital's medical literature search program. He typed in the key words *CMV or cytomegalovirus* and was informed that there were 2,627 articles written since 1985. *Pneumonia* turned up 8,527 articles. Three hundred and forty-eight contained *CMV and pneumonia*. *CMV and pneumonia, and* not *transplant* cut the number to 206. He successively excluded *chemotherapy, drug abuse, AIDS, Human Immunodeficiency Virus,* and HIV; eighty-four articles remained. After scanning a few titles, he also excluded *newborns, animals, diagnositc methods,* and *experimental drugs.* Finally, he excluded *homosexual* and was left with a single article, entitled "Does cytomegalovirus play a role in community-acquired pneumonia?" He called the summary of the article onto the screen, to see that the authors' answer was "no." He was still staring at the screen when Larraby's page beeped him out of his wits.

Montana summarized the situation. Larraby immediately grasped both the gravity of Epps's illness and the likely public-relations problems. "Don't tell anything to anyone. I want you to restrict the people who have contact with him to three or four nurses who won't talk. Send his lab work to an outside lab under a fictitious name. A.N. will handle the logistics. I'll be back tomorrow morning."

MONTANA spent a good part of the day sitting in his office staring at a two-foot-high pile of AIDS articles (three months' worth) and musing at how only two days before he had been so uncomfortable with the possibility of investigating Epps as a TB case. He read and reread the most recent AIDS epidemiology data in *Morbidity and*

*Mortality Weekly Report.* The basic pattern hadn't changed much in the past few years. In the United States, the majority were still gay or bisexual men who had acquired it sexually, and most of the rest were drug addicts who had used contaminated needles. Hemophiliacs who had received contaminated blood products and people who received transfusions from infected donors represented very small numbers.

The largest new group was sexual partners of drug users. There were still relatively few, compared to the tens of thousands of total cases, but although their individual illnesses were neither more nor less tragic than those of the gay men, there was an added worry, because they were the likely link to the community of non-drug-using heterosexuals (the fuse to the bomb that would end American civilization, some feared), and because many of them bore children while they were infected. Many of these children were infected before they were born, and half or more of the infected children developed AIDS within a couple of years. Infected kids fared no better than infected adults. In the northeast, AIDS was fast becoming a disease of the urban poor, a group for whom there were precious few advocates and fewer support systems.

The smallest new group was health-care workers and researchers who acquired it from blood exposures that occurred during patient care or laboratory work. The tiny number of cases had provoked a virtual revolution in the minds and behavior of everyone in the medical system, as evidenced by the EC meeting a few days before.

There was a steady stream of oddball theories making the rounds about transmission through mosquito bites and toilet seats, but no one took them seriously. None of this helped Montana, or Epps.

At four, Montana met Crowe in her office. While they

waited for Belkins, Crowe filled him in on her activities. "I've arranged for five nurses to rotate care for Epps. They're all pros, and they understand the seriousness of his illness and the sensitivity of the situation. They've agreed not to discuss Epps with anyone except the three of us. A courier will take blood samples to a reference lab across town. We're using a fictitious name and hospital ID number, so it shouldn't be possible to trace the blood to Epps. The results are being phoned directly to Dr. Belkins. For the moment, there isn't any role for our public-relations people. Anything else we need?"

"Well, it's probably the best you can do. It's hard to believe anything will keep this business under wraps for long. I guess we'll forgo the caution sticker on the specimen. Don't you think?"

The buzz of A.N.'s intercom interrupted Montana. "We'll be right over," she said into the phone, and turning to Montana, said, "Belkins can't leave Epps. We're meeting him there." It took fifteen minutes to make the three-minute trip to the sixteenth floor since the end-of-the-day rush for the elevators was in full swing.

Belkins was in the conference room adjacent to Epps's room. He was sitting alone at the head of the dining-room-sized table, which was covered with pages of handwritten notes, ribbons of ECG tracings, lab reports, tubes of blood, and little opaque jars. Seeing A.N. and Montana, he slid his tortoise-shell glasses down from the top of his head and twisted the top of his gold Cross pen and laid it on the drug-order sheet he'd been working on.

"He's falling apart. His respiratory rate is thirty-five, his X ray's worse, and his blood gases are terrible." He pushed his glasses back up and picked up a paper clip he'd been torturing as he looked at A.N. "He can't keep breathing at this rate. He's tiring and I don't have any reason to think that we can turn it around

52

soon enough to help him. I'm planning to intubate him as soon as we get the anesthesiologist and the equipment organized. I told the ICU that we'll be taking him down within the hour and that they should have a ventilator ready. Monty, what do you think of trying ganciclovir?"

"It's still experimental, it doesn't work very well, it's toxic, and we'd need to enroll him in a research protocol to get any shipped in, but it could be his only chance. I'll get to work on it. I'll also work on getting some CMV immune globulin.

Montana was detached from the situation just enough to be able to watch the arteries in Crowe's temples begin to pulsate. He couldn't tell whether she was concerned about Epps's decline (possibly) or the logistic problems of caring for him in the fishbowl environment of the intensive care unit (certainly). In her calm efficient way, she began discussing an alternate strategy.

"Dr. Belkins, it would make many things easier if we can keep Mr. Epps here. Tell me what you need, and I'll have it moved."

"I need an ICU."

"Only a small one. I'll make the rest of this floor available to you, if you need. Now tell me who and what you need."

"We need a ventilator, an X-ray machine, a blood-gas analyzer, infusion pumps, transducers for arterial and Swan-Ganz lines, ICU nurses, and a respiratory therapist around the clock. You should also tell Anesthesia to come here to intubate him instead of to the ICU. Oh yes, and get a real good crash cart."

"They'll be here in half an hour." A.N. headed down the stairs toward the ICU.

Belkins propped his elbows on the table and rubbed his eyes without removing his glasses. "He was in trouble when I got here this morning, and he's gotten worse every hour. This morning, I thought the biopsy was a weird fluke. I believe it now, but I still don't understand it."

"Did he tell you anything useful?"

"He really hasn't been able to hold a decent conversation. I told him he has an unusual and serious form of pneumonia, but I haven't been able to get too much from him. He's using every ounce of energy just to breathe."

As the two sat together, they could hear the ventilator being moved from the elevator toward Epps's room. The anesthesiologist stuck his head through the door and said he and his tubes were ready whenever they were. He winked at Montana and disappeared.

Belkins stood up, took off his jacket, rolled up his sleeves, and found his stethoscope under a stack of forms, then turned to Montana. "Can you stay? We might be able to talk to him afterward."

They joined the others in Epps's room. These included the anesthesiologist, a respiratory therapist, a nurse, and Epps's wife, Grace. Belkins began a monologue directed toward Epps. "Van, as I told you earlier, we're going to pass a tube through your nose to help you breathe. The first thing we'll do is spray your nose and throat so you won't feel the tube going in. You won't be able to talk while the tube is in and the machine will help you with each breath. Let it do the work for you. Don't fight it or try to breathe against it. Do you have any questions?"

Epps wasn't in any position to ask questions. He lay with his eyes closed, breathing a mile a minute, with beads of sweat covering his face. He whispered "Okay" and went back to breathing. Belkins asked Mrs. Epps to wait outside. Montana never ceased to marvel at the ease with which planned intubations were consummated, especially since his own attempts to place endotracheal tubes when he was an intern had invariably been hair-raising events. In those days, he was typically resuscitating someone who had stopped breathing and was mostly dead. Invariably, an essential piece of equipment was missing, or it was impossible to stand at the head of the bed, or a denture got knocked into the trachea, or someone was jiggling the target around by pounding on the patient's chest to try to persuade the heart to start beating again. For these and a dozen other reasons, Montana's intubations were harrowing both for him and for the patients, only a few of whom had lived to tell the tale.

But by the time Montana finished thinking about it, Epps was attached to the ventilator. Fortunately, he was able to coordinate his own breathing efforts with the ventilator's. During the next five minutes, his color improved, his blood pressure normalized, and he stopped sweating. He opened his eyes and began to trace shapes in the air with his finger. Belkins handed him a pencil and a clipboard that had a pad of paper with the alphabet already printed on it. Most patients used these like a Ouija board to spell out messages. Epps turned the pad over and drew a full-page question mark.

Belkins resumed his monologue. "You're doing very well. I don't know when you'll be able to get rid of the tube; probably in a couple of days. It depends on how you feel and on what we can learn about what's causing your pneumonia. Let me fill you in on what I've learned so far. Then I need to ask you some questions.

"The pneumonia is caused by a virus called cytomegalovirus. It doesn't usually cause infections in people your age and I'm trying to figure out why it picked you. I've asked my colleague Dr. Montana to join me. He's an infectious disease specialist and I'd like him to hear what you have to say. Is that all right?" Epps nodded.

"Have you had any medical problems that I don't know about?" Epps shook his head from side to side.

"Have you taken any medicines or have you been in contact with any chemicals?" Another shake.

"This will seem a strange question, but I have to ask it. Have you had sex with a man in the last ten years?" At this, Epps ran afoul of the ventilator. The result was a paroxysm of wheezes and puffs that set off the alarms and brought the entire crew back into the room. After peace was restored, Belkins continued, "I take it that's a 'no'?" A nod.

"Prostitute?" Shake.

"Have you ever used drugs?" Epps, clearly feeling much better, rolled his eyes before shaking his head.

"Monty, anything else?"

"Transfusions?"

"I know he hasn't had any." At this point, Epps scribbled "hiplastyear" on his clipboard.

They stared at it for a while, then Montana asked, "hip last year?" Nod.

Belkins looked chagrined. "You know, I really wasn't involved in that hospitalization when he had his hip surgery. He might have received some blood then." Epps was nodding vigorously.

"Van, we're asking these questions because we're looking for an explanation for this pneumonia. I told you it's an unusual one. It might just be bad luck, but it will help to know if something else is going on. Some of the possibilities are pretty unpleasant. One possibility that we need at least to consider is that your transfusion, or something else, could have given you AIDS. That's very unlikely, but it is possible." He paused briefly.

"I know you know a lot about AIDS because your foundation has been supporting research on it. I can't make the prospect any brighter than you know it is. But I want you to realize that it's just an outside possibility at

56

the moment. I'd like to test your blood to see if there's any sign of the virus. I need your consent to get the test. May I go ahead?" Epps looked directly at Belkins and nodded slowly.

"That's it for now. Do you have any questions?" Epps shook his head. "Can I get you anything?" Epps took up his pencil again and printed "CIGAR."

Belkins said, "Maybe tomorrow. See you in the morning. Should I fill Grace in on the things we talked about?" Epps nodded one more time.

The news of the transfusion was a bombshell. Belkins spoke first when they got back to the conference room. "I feel like I'm wearing a goddamn 'kick me' sign. How the hell can I have missed that? It's got to be the answer."

"Maybe, if he has AIDS. Do you believe his other answers?"

"Absolutely. The guy's life is a completely open book. He spends every minute that he's not working with Grace. I've seen them together and can't believe that he'd be involved with anyone else, man or woman."

"Dan, saints were banned from Philadelphia a long time ago. Keep an open mind on the subject. I'll try to find out about the transfusion and find the donor. Call you if I come up with anything."

They separated, Belkins to talk to Grace Epps and then to plot Epps's course for the night, Montana to search out the transfusion history.

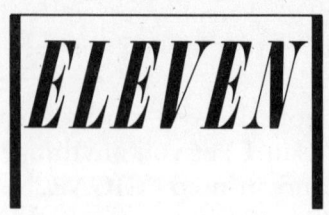

# ELEVEN

THE LOGICAL place to look for a person's transfusion history is in his medical record. By law, this contains all sorts of useful information, including the date and number of transfusions, and a receipt that identifies the specific unit(s) of blood transfused. The system works well when the record is available. On any given day, 15 percent aren't. They are either (a) in clinic, (b) in conference, (c) awaiting dictation, (d) in the warehouse, (e) being microfilmed, (f) in transit, or (g) we don't know. The remarkable thing is that the chart of interest is always part of the 15 percent. Nonetheless, Montana looked for Epps's old record. It wasn't in the nursing station's drawer that was reserved for such documents. The next step was the medical records department. After keeping him on hold for five minutes, the clerk chose option (g). Montana's fallback position was to call the blood bank, which maintained complete and permanent records of its activities. Getting a recorded message of whom to page for an emergency, Montana walked down to the blood bank. It was locked tight and had a sign taped to the door, saying that the tech was at supper and please page her if there was an emergency. Otherwise, she would be back in twenty-five minutes. It was just as well. It was already six o'clock and he was late for day-care pickup again.

Molly already had supper under control when he and the kids arrived. She was at her most efficient. There was a paper napkin at every place and the forks were out *before* the food. "No, we're *not* having company tonight, Jake," she said as she whizzed around the still-clean kitchen (thanks to Mrs. Soame's hard work that morning) distributing the spaghetti and topping it off with the modular sauce that kept everyone happy: Isaac—no mushrooms; Abe—no mushrooms, no onions, no peppers; Jake—anchovies; Montana—no meat, no garlic (unless Molly's having garlic); Whimsy—whatever. They barely got a chance to lick their plates before Molly had them in the dishwasher. She shooed the kids out to play and practice and launched into her researches on the dead men and woman. Starting with their CVs, she had ascertained their places of birth (five from Philly), their secondary education (three from Central High), colleges (heavily Ivy League, but no two from the same place), and medical schools (four Harvard, three Penn). Three had served in the military. Nine had done research fellowships at the National Institutes of Health in Bethesda and six had been there at some point within a five-year period during the early sixties.

"It must be somebody they knew or something they did together at the NIH," she concluded.

"The NIH was a lot more attractive than the army. Just about everybody who was bright enough went there after med school. They didn't call them the yellow berets for nothing. So it's no surprise that most academic docs passed through there early in their careers. Anyway, how would somebody or something from twenty-five years ago hasten their demise?" Montana asked.

"I'm not sure, exactly. You'll have to take it from here."

Montana saw that this investigation had just about run its course and that they were unlikely to discover the explanation for the cluster, in the still-unlikely event the cluster really was more than a chance aggregation. Like many other investigations he'd run, it was time to put this one on the shelf, unless more deaths occurred or new facts turned up. He also was preoccupied with Epps, both the illness and the possibility that the transfusion may have played a role.

Montana told Molly what was going on with Epps. Although they always talked about their work, Molly, being in the blood business herself, had a direct professional interest in the possibility that Epps might have contracted AIDS from a transfusion. Beyond that, this was such incredibly good gossip that he would have told her about it even if she had been a cigar store Indian.

Molly pointed out the obvious. "This will be the biggest media story of the season. If he has AIDS, or even if he only might have AIDS, then everybody from *The New York Review of Books* to *Hustler* is going to give it the twenty-dollar treatment." Molly still thought twenty dollars was a lot of money. "Seems to me you want to know pretty quick whether he got it from a transfusion. You're going to be pretty busy explaining this at press conferences."

Until now, Montana had been treating this mostly as a theoretical problem. But, as usual, Molly was right about the need to know quickly. In fact, Montana was unlikely ever to appear at a press conference, since UHOP employed a raft of public-relations people, who looked and sounded great on TV. On the other hand, Montana was going to be the one to spoon-feed them the information they would need to recite in their impeccably authoritative manner.

The Montanas spent the rest of the evening getting the kids read to, cajoled, and threatened to bed. At nine o'clock they turned in themselves. Montana awoke at four, still pondering Epps. He and Whimsy breakfasted together and at 5:30, Montana whispered to Molly that if she could handle the kids, he would head for the hospital. She nodded without waking.

Half an hour later, Montana was in the blood bank talking to Lorraine, the night tech. He had anticipated either that she would tell him to wait until the day shift arrived or that it would take her forever to trace a possible transfusion whose date was only approximately known. To his surprise, she turned to the computer console, selected number 4 ("search recipient's history") from the menu of options, and typed in Epps's medical record number. Within thirty seconds, it listed seven blood products assigned to Epps, with dates for each. The last two were units that had been typed in the past two days and held for use if an emergency occurred during the bronchoscopy. The earlier five coincided with his admission of the year before. At that point, she turned the keyboard over to Montana and told him that she'd be available if he needed help, backhandedly assuring him that the system was idiotproof. He settled into Lorraine's chair and stared into the green glow. It prompted him to enter the numbers of the units of interest. He indicated the earlier five and watched the display give him detailed information about each. Three of the units hadn't been used but had merely been available as standby for the surgery. The other two had both been transfused on the same day, presumably during surgery. Once again at the computer's prompt, he indicated the two units that had been transfused and watched it display the source of those units.

Montana expected to see the names of two donors, whom he would need to track down, probably with the help of the state epidemiologist. Instead, it listed Epps's name twice. Montana started over but ended up in the same place. He called Lorraine.

"I'm trying to list the donors of these units, but it keeps giving me the recipient."

Lorraine bent over him and repeated the sequence. Once again, "Epps" popped onto the screen. "Epps was the donor," she said, straightening up. Seeing the blank look on Montana's face, she went on. "Epps was part of our autologous transfusion program." At that point, Montana understood, but she continued, figuring he might be as naive as he looked. "Healthy patients donate a unit or two of their own blood a month or so before elective surgery. We hold it in case they need a transfusion during surgery. It's a lot safer than other blood since there isn't any chance of a transfusion reaction. I remember when Epps came in before his operation. Everyone made a big fuss about him. There was a lot of joking about whether his blood would be blue and whether we could raffle it off if he didn't use it."

This all made perfect sense, but it was also a dead end. Unpleasant as the prospect was, the transfusion was the logical explanation as the source of Epps's AIDS (Montana had given up thinking that there would be another explanation). But the man couldn't have given himself AIDS. Autotransfusion was the same as no transfusion, for these purposes. Montana thanked Lorraine and left, shaking his head at the near miss.

Montana had entered the hospital through a service entrance in the rear. On his way to the elevators, he passed the main entrance and saw clusters of lights, video vans, and reporters talking into microphones.

Absentmindedly kicking at a bloodstain in the carpet, he stared at the numbers flashing over the elevator and reflected on Epps's "conversation" of the previous night. The man's command of situations was truly extraordinary. Notwithstanding the fact that he was critically ill, had just been told he might have AIDS, and couldn't talk, he put his physicians at ease by joking about a cigar. Epps would probably enjoy knowing that in Montana's day, interns referred to endotracheal tubes that were inserted through the mouth as "big red cigars." Now the interns called them "big white cigars." Modern times, modern medicine, modern materials.

Like Halley's comet, UHOP's elevators always traveled great distances before making their next appearance: 9, 10, 11, 12, 14, 15, 16, 17, 18.

# TWELVE

17, 16, 15, 14, 12, 11, 10, 9, 8, 7, 6, 5, 4, 3, 2, 1, B, open, step in, beep. Montana's beeper paged him to a phone on Epps's floor, so he went there directly. The elevator opened onto a dense phalanx of security guards, who hustled him back onto the elevator as soon as he set foot off it.

He got off on the seventeenth floor and called downstairs. A.N. answered the phone herself. "Montana, I'm sorry to call you at this hour. Can you get here as soon as possible?"

"I tried to get there thirty seconds ago, but the bouncers thought I was underage."

"I'll wait for you."

"Meet me at the stairs."

A.N. was standing in the stairwell when he arrived. Her hair in its usual orderly twist, she still looked fresh in yesterday's six-hundred-dollar Dior suit, although a more trained eye than Montana's would notice the slight bagging in the elbows, the creases in the skirt, and a little droop in the silk tie. She did notice that his hair didn't lie flat and that he was wearing rumpled corduroys, a blue Oxford cloth button-down drip-dry shirt that didn't quite live up to the "never needs ironing" claim, and a fourteen-year-old Harris tweed jacket. She'd been in her outfit all night; Montana was fresh from a shower. She escorted him down the hall.

"Dan says he's not doing well. The press also knows something is up. The place is lousy with reporters. The three of us need to talk."

Belkins emerged from Epps's room at their approach. His fine red stubble made him appear pale and uncharacteristically disheveled. This was his second night in a row up with Epps, and he had abandoned his normal clothes for hospital scrubs. It occurred to Montana that they should make coffee-colored scrubs for occasions such as these.

"He turned sour around three this morning." Montana thought of Molly as he looked at Belkins's puffy transparent pinkish lids. Red heads don't do well without sleep. "He's a lot worse now. I've tried just about everything, but he's losing ground. He's been comatose for the past two hours. Learn anything useful, Monty?"

"Not really. I tracked down his transfusion. He received two units of his own blood during his hip surgery. That doesn't get us any closer to an explanation."

A.N. spoke next. "We're going to have to hold a press conference. When will his HIV serology results be ready?"

Montana answered. "It's a two-step test. The first phase, the ELISA, will be out today. It's a screening test. If it's negative, we stop. If it's positive, they'll do a Western blot to confirm it. That'll take a few days, even for a V.I.P."

"What about that five-minute test?" she asked.

"It's also a screening test. It won't tell us anything more than the ELISA does. Since we sent the sample late yesterday, there wasn't any reason to prefer it. It's also harder to get without drawing special attention to the patient."

Belkins proposed a statement indicating only that Epps was suffering from a severe case of pneumonia. They were working on the wording when they heard the alarm ring in Epps's room and one of the nurses came barreling into the conference room. She mumbled "arrest," and Belkins and Montana sprinted after her into Epps's room.

His cardiac monitor showed a scribble where an organized heartbeat should have been. A nurse was kneeling on the bed, rocking back and forth, pumping on Epps's chest, trying to keep some blood flowing. The respiratory tech was squeezing the black oxygen bag attached to Epps's endotracheal tube in a wheezy counterpoint to the rhythm of the cardiac massage. Belkins pushed two ampoules of bicarb into the IV, reached into the crash cart and pulled out two electric paddles, one that looked like a small breadboard, the other like something from a laser tag game. He squirted a worm of clear greenish electrode paste on each paddle, pushed the big one under Epps, and pressed the other one over Epps's heart. Everybody backed off at the count of three and Belkins pulled the trigger. The jolt lifted Epps off the bed. The bagging and pumping resumed. They reconnected the monitor, which settled down into its former chaotic picture.

They shocked Epps four more times. On the third try, something approaching a normal beat appeared for fifteen seconds, but the jumble, known as ventricular fibrillation, returned. They tried a pharmacopoeia of exotic compounds, none of which had the slightest effect. Not the ones that usually work, not the ones that sometimes work, not the ones that hardly ever work. After ten minutes, even the scribble subsided, leaving only a weakly meandering line on the monitor. Belkins injected adrenaline directly into the heart, hoping to stimulate some electrical activity. After that, they put a needle into the pericardium to see if any blood had collected that might be compressing the heart. Finally, they inserted a wire into the heart and attached it to an electrical pacer. This, too, failed, leaving them after forty minutes with no more options.

"Time," called Belkins. One of the nurses read the time in the same voice as the lady who says "at the tone, the time will be. . . ." "That will be all," Belkins said. "Thank you for your efforts." He walked around the bed and clicked off the monitor and the ventilator. Everyone present except Crowe had participated in scores of similar failed resuscitations, but none of them had ever made peace with this part. Montana was struck by the tableau: a motionless patient, surrounded by motionless doctors, nurses, and technicians, none of whom looked at one another. The scene lasted only a second. The technician disconnected the ventilator. The nurses began to remove the tubes, lines, and wires that Epps had acquired during the preceding day.

Belkins left the room to find Grace Epps. Montana and A.N. spoke briefly, then A.N. went off to organize what would now be an enormous press conference announcing Epps's unexpected death from an unusually severe and fulminant case of pneumonia.

Montana went for a walk in the rain.

# *THIRTEEN*

EPPS'S DEATH caused an enormous ruckus. UHOP and Epps's own public-relations office held news conferences and issued press releases. UHOP's presentations were highly professional and accurate, if incomplete. As planned, they announced that Epps had a viral pneumonia, "similar to the flu," and that a series of complications led to his death.

The death was the lead story on every network's nightly news. Although Epps was a private citizen, his funeral was an international event. Five governments, the World Health Organization, UNICEF, and the World Bank sent representatives. The Vice-President and senior clergy from all major faiths came. Celebrities and monarchs came from fourteen countries. The networks covered the funeral. The paparazzi shadowed Grace Epps. There was a tremendous surge in the number of people seeking flu vaccine.

Montana followed the coverage of the Epps story with a combination of morbid curiosity and free-floating anxiety. He was always fascinated to see how the media portrayed events or people or subjects he knew personally. Visiting a friend at Columbia in the Spring of 1968, he saw the police hack up the furniture in the university president's office after they had arrested the protesting students who had been sitting-in there for days. The next morning he read in the *Times* how the students had destroyed the office. This time, the coverage was pretty accurate. Along with the usual who, what, and where about the man and the funeral, Charlayne Hunter-Gault did an interesting interview with an economist from Harvard who specialized in estate-tax legislation. Charles Kuralt did a travelogue-type piece on the exotic places such as Hong King and Singapore whose names were attached to the various strains of flu. But with all the bits in *Time, Newsweek, People,* on "All Things Considered," "Wall Street Week," and CNN, there was nothing from "60 Minutes," nothing from the *National Enquirer,* and no leak about Epps's HIV-antibody test, which had indeed been positive.

Montana was pretty busy with day-to-day hospital epidemiology problems. A maintenance crew disassembled an operating room table to fix one of its cranks. When they turned over the top, they found the underside caked with dried blood and studded with wads of dried chewing gum. Closer inspection revealed the wads to be clusters of maggots. For the classical-minded, this was an example of the wheel coming full circle. In olden times, maggots were introduced into wounds to clean out the pus. Carola, who was representing the Epidemiology Unit in the operating rooms at the time, was not amused by the historical precedent, despite her renewed interest in high-necked white Victorian lace blouses and brooches of woven tresses. She spent hours inspecting other nooks and crannies and coaxing the OR staff back to work. The OR staff gave her a basket of rotten fruit to commemorate the event.

Through it all, Montana continued to fret about the transfusions that hadn't caused Epps's death. When a free morning cropped up, he called the blood bank and got the director, Dr. Rudolph Low, on the phone. "Ru, can we have lunch sometime? I need your advice. My treat."

Low was a friendly, if socially inept, man who never hesitated to answer the main phone in the lab when the secretary was busy and who prided himself on being able to identify most of the medical staff by the "hello." In an institution full of egos and agendas, Low's mission was clearly and refreshingly service to patients and their doctors. He also weighed three hundred pounds in his birthday suit, and could be counted on for meetings that included food. "Today's free. I'll meet you at eleven thirty at the new cheesesteak stand in the Ninth Street market."

Montana arrived to find Low taking up an entire bench at an outdoor table, munching away on steak covered with melted Cheez Whiz. A lean-to of packing cartons protected him from the wind. The sandwich looked small in his beefy hands, and he had already taken a big toll in fresh grease stains on his light-blue double-knit jacket and painfully short red and navy striped tie. Napkins swirled about him. "You have to try this stuff, it's a giant step for mankind." Low waxed eloquent about fast food. Still a bachelor at forty-six, he'd become a steak and cheese gourmet when his mother had died four years before. She had been a big woman, too.

Thinking almost anything was justified in a good cause, Montana ordered a sandwich, sat facing Low, and sipped from his can of Canfield's chocolate fudge diet soda. Now, a decent diet soda really was a giant step. While waiting for Montana's steak and Low's refill, they compared notes on the 76ers. Neither followed sports as a rule, but it was impossible to ignore Philadelphia's premier team. Like every other physician in the country, they had nursed a secret envy of their colleagues named Joel or Jeff or any other J name that allowed them to be called Dr. J. Now that the real Dr. J. had retired, they commiserated with one another. The prospect of years of domination by the Celtics was almost more than strong men could bear.

"Ru, it looks as though Molly might need to have her knee fixed after the fall rowing season ends. Her orthopod at UHOP told her she might need a transfusion during the procedure and that she should bank some of her own blood. She has a bunch of questions but almost as much anxiety about asking as she does about going to the dentist. Do you mind if I ask you for her?"

"Not as long as you're paying for lunch." The breeze lifted the long hairs that had been carefully arranged to cover his top.

"How far ahead of time can she donate her own blood?"

"We like it to be four weeks before the surgery. That gives her body time to replenish the blood she donated, and the banked blood is still reasonably fresh."

"She's planning to row in the Turkey Day Regatta. Could she donate even earlier, so she'll be in shape for the race?"

"We can make an exception for her and freeze it; then she can donate whenever. Montana, why are you asking me this stuff? Molly's a terrific hematologist and knows as much about transfusion medicine as anybody else in the city, even if she doesn't run a blood blank."

"I'm really a terrible liar," Montana lied. "You know how people fixate on problems with things they know the most about. She really wants to know if there's any chance she could get the wrong unit of blood."

"None." For the first time, he put his sandwich down on the paper plate pinned to the table under his elbow. "UHOP's patients are probably the safest in the world. My one claim to fame is the fail-safe system I designed with the computerniks."

"How does it work?" Montana was eating around the steak. The onions and roll were great.

"We've known for a long time that the major source of transfusion accidents is clerical error in typing the identification numbers on labels or misreading the numbers. Our system eliminates both possibilities for error. When Molly comes in to donate, we call up her profile on the computer. The computer generates the label for the blood bag on the spot. It includes all of her identifiers, including her medical record and social security number. The label is printed in regular text and in bar-code format that machines can read. When we type the blood and test it for hepatitis and HIV, those results also get directly imprinted on the label. When we cross match it for a recipient, in Molly's case herself, the recipient's ID number and bar code are also imprinted on the label as well as the result of the cross match. When we actually pull out a unit to give to a patient, we use a laser scanner to read all of the bar codes, just like they do at the A&P. It completely does away with the possibility of human error. The computer checks that the blood passed all of the tests, that it hasn't outdated, that the donor's name hasn't appeared on any deferral lists, and that the cross match was okay. Finally, the computer console displays the name of the recipient and prints the name and ID number in big letters on the bag. That way we're sure we give out the right unit, and the folks who give it to the patient can be sure which patient is supposed to get it. I've been trying to talk the administration into putting bar codes on patients' wristbands and to put bar-code readers on all of the clinical units. That would eliminate the last possiblity of human error—giving the blood to the wrong person. All you'd need to do is scan the patients' wristband and the unit of blood in sequence. The computer would then clear you to proceed with the transfusion.

"You know," Low continued, two minutes and twenty-three seconds since he last took a bite, "the AIDS scare was the driving force for a lot of the increased safety measures. But ever since we started screening donated blood for HIV in eighty-five, that's just about disappeared. The only way we'd miss an infectious unit is if the infected donor hadn't started to make antibody yet. It's a negligible chance. Most of the transfusion-associated AIDS cases we're seeing now come from transfusions that occurred before we started screening. But AIDS was never the major risk of transfusion anyway. So, we've gone in the right direction mostly for the wrong reason. Any port in a storm."

Montana was doubly impressed. First, the system really was as close to airtight as it could be. "Sounds as though you spent a fair amount of time on that system."

"Only about five years of my life." This sounded right to Montana, who had wrestled with computer-based surveillance systems. The things that seemed obvious never were.

The other thing, which he couldn't comment on to Low, was that Epps's transfusion had occurred after the blood bank had started routinely screening donated units for HIV antibody. In theory, there shouldn't have *been* any units of infected blood around to be substituted, even if a mistake had been made. That seemed to make an already remote possibility even less likely.

"Molly will be impressed as all get out. I don't think they have anything nearly so sophisticated at her shop. She'll be a lot more relaxed about the operation." He pushed his bench away from the table and wiped his hands.

"My pleasure. Give her my regards. I'd like to come and watch the regatta." He mustered enough self-control not to reach for Montana's plate of naked steak. "Do you think we should check out the Tofutti place next door?"

# FOURTEEN

MONTANA AND Low walked back to UHOP together, the midday sun compensating for the cool weather. When Montana got to his office, he took his bike down from its hook on the wall and headed for the river. This was one of the days that Molly rowed during her lunch hour. He needed to sort out some of the things Low had told him, and he might as well do that at the river.

When he got to Boathouse Row, he checked in at the Philadelphia Girls' Rowing Club boathouse to find that Molly's shell was out. She had started rowing at PGRC when she really was a girl and it was the only club that allowed women to row. She had remained with the club during the ensuing years, even though a lot of other clubs invited her to row for them. In college, she had attained moderate notoriety, first as the stroke of the national champion women's eight and then as a singles rower. By the time she entered med school, she regularly beat most of the men on the river and had won several international events, including the Henley regatta. Since then, the demands of adulthood had limited her competitive rowing, although at the moment she was toying with the idea of entering the national master's competition. She maintained an active recreational interest in the sport at all times and had recently become a member of PGRC's board of governors.

Montana and Molly first met each other on the water. He had been a year ahead of her at Penn but was in the physics-for-peace–poetry–Russian history–underground press circle, which intersected not at all with her rowing-for-peace–folksong–English lit–artist commune circle—except for the Skimmer weekend when Montana's thermodynamics class (Physics 6.63) launched its solar-powered turbo raft, Maxwell's Demon, with Montana as captain and crew. He says he was the only one in a position to help her when the ZBT beer-can yacht caught her shell in its wake and dunked her into the river. Molly remembers it differently. She was practicing for a meet when she saw his floating physics lab sink out of sight. Montana's pockets were so loaded with wrenches, screwdrivers, solder, and rheostats that he was going down like a stone. She jumped out and swam him to the nearby keg boat. Although they didn't renew their acquaintance, or appreciate each other's special qualities until they met again in medical school, the Montanas still exchanged bits of flotsam on special occasions.

But Molly wasn't a fitness buff. When the first tentative inklings of romance quickened in the dissecting lab, Montana was disappointed that she never wanted to join him for a bike ride, jog, game of squash, or even a walk in the country. At first, he thought she just wasn't interested in him. But he soon found out that her favorite place was in bed. Montana thought he could be happy with that arrangement, but he learned that she was happiest amid pillows and quilts, whether he was there or not. Much later, when he met Molly's mother, Isadora, at the family home in Weston, Massachusetts, he learned that as a girl Molly never played field hockey or hiked with her friends in the White Mountains, or even sailed with the kids at their summer home on Nantucket. She stayed with her pillows and quilts, in a hammock, on a porch, at the beach, or on her bed, depending on the weather, the location, and hour. Isadora still didn't know where the rowing came from. Montana was convinced that it was basically a training program for the future Olympic napping competition.

Montana moved along up the river past the statuary and under the Strawberry Mansion bridge. That was always a dangerous passage, since about a thousand pigeons roost under it. He spotted her rowing away from him toward the head of the course. She had the apparently effortless stroke that betrayed years of training. She saw him standing on the riverbank and waved before bringing the shell around. Then she took off down the river at thirty strokes a minute. Montana watched as she approached, passed him, and then receded until she was lost to sight. He turned his thoughts back to Epps.

His professional involvement in the Epps case was really finished. He had thoroughly investigated the possibility that Epps's AIDS had been acquired in the hospital. And it was clear that it couldn't have been. Montana knew none of the hospital's personnel had a needlestick or extensive exposure to Epps; therefore no one needed to know the diagnosis, the hospital's new notification policy notwithstanding. He was left with the sense of dissonance that came with trying to fit Epps into one of the other risk groups. It just didn't feel right. Epps's life really had seemed an open book for decades. He was too tempting a target for the muckrakers not to have discovered his secrets if he had any. Nobody had ever bothered writing an unauthorized biography, presumably because there wasn't anything juicy to say. Anyway, if he'd been using IV drugs, he would have had the sense and the connections to get clean needles.

That really only left sexual, probably homosexual, contact. Montana knew he shouldn't be surprised that even the most respectable closets sometimes had skeletons in them. Maybe Epps had the consummate discreet partners. Maybe he had paid off the muckrakers. Maybe Montana should get back to doing real work.

# FIFTEEN

MONTANA'S BEEPER went off as he passed the front of Rocky's Museum of Art and again as he pedalled down the Ben Franklin Parkway. He switched it off when it sang a third time within two hundred yards. Ten minutes later, as he coasted up to UHOP's front door, he saw an armada of media vans that made all previous news coverage look like the opening of an elementary school in Bucks County. There were at least fifty trailers with antennae on their roofs and fat black coaxial cables snaking toward the hospital. Anchorpersons were jostling for position in front of UHOP's distinctive main entrance. Montana surmised that (a) this blitz probably had something to do with Epps, (b) it probably wasn't good news, and (c) his beeper's paroxysms were most likely related to this invasion. He wended his way to his office, noting for once the value of his remote location. Arriving there and finding an assistant vice-president camped outside his door, he knew he had been right on all three counts.

"Dr. M., there's a lot of commotion about Mr. Epps at the hospital. Dr. Larraby said I should ask you to meet him in his office right away." Assistant VPs came in several models. This one was your basic tape recorder. It could deliver a message. It could also fetch. Montana was going to have to accompany this fine specimen back to UHOP. He hung his bike from the hook on his office wall, put on his white coat, and set out with Sancho Panza. They ducked in through the dumpsters' loading bay and made their way through the hazardous waste decontamination area. Montana noted the needles poking through the cardboard boxes and plastic bags awaiting dispatch to a nearby dump that served as both kids' playground and addicts' materials resource center.

Montana wasn't exactly sure what a high dudgeon was, but Larraby seemed to be in one. He had every vice-president, several members of the board, and Belkins stuffed into the board room and he was pacing between marble busts. Montana took the only remaining chair, one of the high-backed leather models with a carved eight-pointed star and beams of light on the headrest. While Larraby pursued a one-sided interrogation of Daren Ang, Montana reflected on the furnishings of the room. Intended, like the rest of UHOP, to be a sleek contemporary facility, it had acquired bits and pieces of the hospital's three parent institutions, all of which had been designed at least seventy-five years earlier. Solid dark mahogany abutted light fruitwood veneer. Muttonchopped benefactors in marble glowered at abstract prints. In addition to the chairs and busts from the Star of Bethlehem Hospital (the SOB for short), there was the mahogany conference table from Franklin Municipal Hospital, and a ten-foot-high brass stork that had once soared, bundle in beak, across the courtyard of the Women's Charitable Institution.

"How many people knew Epps had AIDS?" Larraby asked.

"Only Dr. Belkins, Dr. Montana, Ms. Crowe, and I knew for sure." Ang's voice trembled slightly. "But the nurses who took care of Epps should have known, and the X-ray tech might have overheard something. And I suppose a lot of other people knew, since Dr. Montana's team notifies all the labs and support services who has AIDS." The man was positively beaming. Here he was, completely off the hook.

Montana spoke up. "I delayed implementation of the notification rule. I assumed you wouldn't object." He paused, looked at Larraby, who remained silent, and continued. "The story doesn't have to have been leaked. I've been expecting this since he died. Even a moderately motivated reporter should have been able to figure it out. On the one hand, we have a man dying unexpectedly and the hospital giving out a lot of mumbo jumbo about 'unusual' pneumonia. On the other hand, the main reference lab in the city has a blood test for a nonexistent patient at our hospital. I've been able to get results from them by phone without any difficulty. No reason why a reporter can't call up and identify himself as a UHOP lab administrator and wheedle the information out of them. A half hour's telephoning could have accomplished it."

Larraby dismissed everyone but Belkins, Crowe, and Montana, whom he ushered into his office. Montana had never quite seen this expression on Larraby before. He wasn't nervous or angry. The man seemed hurt. He sat for the first time.

"I worked with Van Epps for over twenty years. He was one of the best friends UHOP or I had. This is a tragedy of classic proportions." He stood, turned his back toward the group, briefly gazed out the window, then faced them again and half-sat on the edge of his desk. Looking at Montana, he said, "This puts our last EC meeting in a very different light. It's much clearer to me now that the hospital has a responsibility not to bend to unreasonable fears. Perhaps his death will contribute to a more rational discussion of the disease." Then to all three of them: "I'm going to address that horde from the fourth estate in half an hour. I assume they will want to know how he got the disease. What other tidbits are they likely to have gleaned from our leakproof staff?"

A.N. replied, "Dr. Belkins and I went through his whole chart this morning. There's nothing in it that casts any doubts on Epps's background or character or suggests in any way that he was gay or used drugs."

Belkins added, "And there weren't any discussions among the people who actually cared for him. I was there the whole time."

"Then UHOP doesn't need to be involved in any speculation about some tawdry history," Larraby said.

"A reporter might know that Epps received a blood transfusion here about a year ago and suggest that as a possible source of AIDS," Montana volunteered. "But I checked on it and it was an autologous transfusion, so it should be fairly easy to deal with the question if it arises. There will probably be some question about whether the blood bank could have given him the wrong unit." Montana would have gone on to explain his conversation with Low when Larraby broke in.

"Thanks for letting me know about the transfusion. Dr. Low tells me our blood bank is one of the best in the country. I'm sure it will stand up to any scrutiny." He rose as he ended the discussion, addressing his final remarks to Montana and Belkins. "Be sure to let A.N. know if you come across anything else." He left them in his office as he strode back to the board room, now packed to the rafters with network news reporters.

Montana, Belkins, and Crowe flipped on the TV in Larraby's office and settled in to watch the show. The shows, actually, since they switched from station to station, finding a different feed on each one. Larraby opened the news conference with a succinct but compassionate summary of AIDS as a problem in society as a whole. He continued with a quiet but moving statement about his personal loss at the death of Epps, not only a benefactor of the hospital but a close personal friend. He spoke of the irony that Epps should have died from AIDS, since he had been so generous in his support of research to find a cure for it, and he concluded with the hope that Epps's foundation support might still lead to a cure. Throughout, he was dignified, understated, and eminently quotable. Epps emerged as a martyr with an unblemished reputation. Only a cad or a Neanderthal would dare broach the possibility of what Larraby had mentioned minutes before, a tawdry past.

As expected, virtually all of the questions dealt with just such issues—"risk factors." Larraby handled these with aplomb. He noted the absence of firm data, indicated that more information was being sought, gave the impression that it would be provided if it was discovered, showed no hint of any impropriety or scandal associated with the diagnosis, and allayed any concern that AIDS had somehow spread out of its usual risk groups and into the general population. He also preempted any questions about the blood transfusion by noting the great care taken by blood banks in general and UHOP's in particular.

At the conclusion of the news conference, Montana shook his head in admiration and looked up Bella and Carola, who joined him in the cafeteria for a quick meeting over frozen yogurt. Carola discussed her handling of a plastic surgeon who took off his mask and gown after completing a lengthy rejuvenation of a very jowly and wealthy chief executive officer, only to discover that his own face was covered with chicken pox.

Montana made his way back to the lab, picked up the three pounds of manuscripts he had been dragging back and forth to work for the past week, and stowed them on his bike. He made his way to the day-care center, where he waited while Isaac and Abe finished smearing their afternoon snack on the sand table, and then while they used the peewee-sized urinal, and then while they donned their hatsmittensglovesscarvesandcoats. All this time they protested that they didn't want to go home early because they would miss their turn to clean the rabbit's cage. Montana solved the impasse by agreeing to take the rabbit home for the weekend. He loaded Abe on the front carrier, Isaac and the bunny on the back carrier, and set course for home, the setting sun glinting off their bike helmets.

# SIXTEEN

MOLLY MET them at the door, helped extricate the kids, and held them up for Whimsy to wash. Between smooches she said, "You should see what's on TV. Cable news showed the whole press conference. Larraby did an incredible job. I think Epps is going to be nominated for sainthood or honorary Mummer."

The kids yammered off to their rooms until supper, which was pizza, in honor of Whimsy's having eaten the chicken that had been defrosting on the countertop. Montana handed the kids the keys to the video game and put Jake in charge so he and Molly could watch the evening news shows.

Larraby's serving as the hospital's spokesman had

proven to be a brilliant maneuver on UHOP's part. Because of him, the focus of the coverage was not on the transfusion as Molly had predicted. The transfusion didn't even make any of the network news shows. Instead, a short intro led into a two-minute clip of Larraby's eulogy of Epps. There were follow-up stories dealing with the ongoing efforts of Epps's charitable foundations, including the AIDS research that they were sponsoring, and also of the general status of AIDS—so many tens of thousand of deaths, so many hundreds of thousands of cases in the pipeline.

Larraby appeared for a newsmaker interview on the "McNeil/Lehrer Newshour." Larraby used the opportunity to stress the need for tolerance and sympathy for those who were infected, for levelheadedness in the formulation of public policy, and for more research on prevention and therapy.

To Judy's question about risk factors, Larraby responded that the risk factors in general were well known, that Epps's character was beyond reproach, and that the cause in this case was not yet known. When Jim Lehrer broke in to press the point, Larraby intimated that Epps could possibly have been exposed in the course of visiting an AIDS research laboratory whose work he had funded.

"What a crock," said Montana and Molly together. Laboratory-acquired AIDS occurred very rarely. In every case, it was the result of either an accident or intensive handling of cell cultures containing astronomically high concentrations of virus. There wasn't any reasonable chance that Epps could have gotten it just by touring a lab.

"On the other hand," said Montana, "he certainly didn't get it from a toilet seat."

"What about his transfusion?" asked Molly.

"I paid six dollars and twenty-five cents for Ru Low's lunch checking that out today. He claims the system is airtight, foolproof, and idiotproof. From what he says, I think he's right. Epps didn't get it that way. Our hero, my dear, must have had feet of clay. That leaves us as the only two pure souls in Philadelphia."

"Just remember what happened to him," muttered Molly as she zapped the remote control to find more news. "And, by the way, I heard Carola's got some unexplained swollen glands, if you catch my drift."

"No, I'm quite sure she doesn't," Montana replied. This comment actually prompted Molly to whip her head around, before she realized she'd been one-upped. It didn't happen often, so it was doubly sweet for Montana when he pulled it off.

Whimsy took Montana for a walk, during which the latter imagined he heard the great rumor mills of the nation groaning in the night air. After the Drs. Montana put the kids to bed, they continued to watch the unfolding of an American melodrama. Epps was mentioned in the monologue of the "Tonight Show" (hosted by nobody in particular), and he was the subject of most of "Nightline." Ted Koppel laid the issue bare but didn't quite articulate the stark choice between illicit drug use and extramarital sex, especially homosexual sex as the cause of Epps's disease. The whole business gave promise of being the hottest story since Teddy Kennedy's famous midnight ride on Martha's Vineyard.

Later that week, Epps appeared on his last *Time* magazine cover (with a question mark over his head) and became the first man ever to appear on a *Penthouse* cover (with a tarnished halo). The supermarket weeklies devoted whole issues to Epps. Men and women who had never been within twenty miles of Epps filed suit against his estate claiming he had had sex with them and hadn't warned them he was contagious.

Although the public din remained at high volume, the Montanas gradually gave up following the Byzantine fabrications and resumed their usual activities. But the affair still received daily attention in the Montana household, with Molly being mildly amused and Montana moderately sad at the carnival atmosphere that had taken hold.

Two weeks after Epps' death, a black-bordered envelope appeared in the Montanas' letterbox. Molly waited to open it in his presence. Vindication.

---

UNIVERSITY OF PENNSYLVANIA

PHILADELPHIA, OCTOBER 7

TO MEMBERS OF THE FACULTY AND STAFF:

With great regret I inform you of the death of:

VANNING EPPS

PAST PRESIDENT, BOARD OF TRUSTEES, which occurred on the thirtieth ultimo, in the fifty-eighth year of his age.

Your obedient servant,

BAYARD HARPEN
President

---

Molly got out the recipe box, but before adding Epps's card to the stack, she laid out the last year's deaths again in the same side-by-side-columns shape Montana had used weeks before. Montana observed that she had added two index cards with Magic Marker–blackened borders as surrogates for Orenberg and Rus, the non-Penn deaths they had discovered in the telephone books. She had obviously spent time by herself thinking about their cluster.

"Looks bad," she said.

*84*

"Looks are probably deceiving," Montana answered, somewhat testily. "I don't think Epps has anything to do with the rest of them. It's a fluke that he gets a card anyway."

Molly put the cards away and would have let the subject drop. To her amazement, Montana extracted from his briefcase a set of cards that corresponded to her own. These, however, were not engraved, and they showed considerable wear and tear. Five by eight inches, narrow ruled, and covered on both sides with scribbled notes in inks of various colors, each summarized their investigation of one of the dead Pennsylvanians, Epps excepted.

"My, my, what have we here?"

"The sum of what we've learned about the departed. Where they lived, who they knew, what they did, and what their hobbies were. Your astute observation about the NIH doesn't appear to be the key. They were there in different years, worked in different buildings, on different projects, with different supervisors and collaborators. The thing that's really striking is that they really don't have anything in common."

Montana shuffled the deck, looking over the notes. "I wonder if we should be looking at their futures instead of their pasts."

"They don't have any futures. Unless you're referring to the Big University in the Sky."

On most nights, Montana would have gone off with her on this conversational detour, constructing an afterlife in which tenured faculty went directly to Heaven and junior staff went to Purgatory to await promotion. And teach a few courses while they waited. This time he kept to the topic at hand.

"Exactly my point. They used to have futures here, but some of them weren't worth having."

"For instance?"

"For instance, Loren Asker. First, the Feds pulled the plug on implantable heart programs all over the country, and he lost big bucks in the process. Then, he petitioned UHOP to make it up, on the grounds that the publicity attracted lots of referrals. He made the pitch to the board of trustees and they turned him down on the spot—on the night he drove into the truck."

"Suicide?" Molly stopped fiddling with the drawstring on her hooded sweatshirt.

"No note left behind, but the man had made that turn many, many times before. I shouldn't think the rain would have made that big a difference. Keep it in mind. Because both Charlotte North and that Orenberg fellow had similarly iffy accidents. Does it seem a little strange to you that a onetime collegiate swimmer should drown in calm water? Does it seem more than a little strange that a psychiatrist who invented a new form of electric shock therapy should electrocute himself with his own machine while administering the treatment to one of his patients?"

"Not to put too fine a point on it, you think all three were suicides. Any idea why?"

"Well, they were soft money heroes. Their careers depended on funds that could dry up anytime. Times are tough. Maybe they were having funding trouble. I'll see how they were doing."

"How will you do that? The NIH only announces the grants it funds."

"I have a friend in Grants and Contracts."

"Do you think your friend will be able to explain all the other deaths—how Roy Davis's heart stopped beating, why Jordan Wicks's ulcerative colitis flared, when—"

Montana cut her off as she was building momentum. "One thing at a time. Meet me here tomorrow."

# *SEVENTEEN*

"FORGET TONIGHT, let's have lunch." Montana was shouting into a pay phone.

"Can't," Molly said. "I have an experiment to run. Where are you calling from? I can barely hear you."

"Broad Street. I've been out doing shoe-leather epidemiology. Put your experiment in the refrigerator. You really want to hear what I found out this morning."

"Will you take me to that sandwich place?"

Thirty minutes later, he watched in horror as she wrapped her long supple fingers and lightly calloused palms around steak and Cheez Whiz. Montana nursed his soda.

"This is great. Are you sure you don't want one?"

Montana didn't bother with an answer. He extracted his cards and started to sort them.

Molly extended her hand and crooked a greasy index finger. "Let me see them."

"They're too messy and so are you. I'll read to you. Charlotte North, who had won award after accolade for her successful drug detox program had lost her federal funding. She would have had to close down in three months." He paused. Molly raised her right eyebrow and kept on eating. "Our former colleague, Professor Orenberg, had recently become the subject of an NIH investigation into possible fraudulent reporting of research

**87**

results. He had been unable to produce many of the records that were requested."

Molly wrestled the cards from his hand and quickly examined them, front and back. "These really are a mess. What else is on here?"

"Well, Roy Davis lost a six-million-dollar grant from the National Cancer Institute. It's unlikely there would have been a cancer lab for him to head for much longer."

"Any more?"

"One. Cigna canceled Jordan Wicks's five-year contract to do stress-reduction training for its employees."

"That's pretty good for a morning's work. What are you going to do next?"

"I figure we're on a roll. I'll see if anything important was going on for the other ones. Office of legal counsel. Vice-president for new business ventures. That kind of stuff." Montana's Adam's apple bobbed up and down when he was excited.

"How are you going to do that?"

"I'll ask around."

"You must have a lot of friends."

"Well, I'm no Bella," Montana said modestly. He brushed a fleck of cheese from her cheek. "But I've pulled a few irons out of various people's fires."

She dropped him off at UHOP with an onion-laden kiss and headed back to her test tubes. That evening, Montana laid out the rest of his day's inquiries, beginning with his cards. In place of the dog-eared cards to which Molly had added a greasy thumbprint at lunch, these were crisp new ones, each of which had only a few lines of neatly typed information—name, cause of death, professional activity, and hot news.

**Asker**
   Drove into oncoming traffic.
   Headed implantable heart program.

Federal funding eliminated abruptly nationwide. Trustees refused contingency support on night of accident.

## North
Drowned in Bimini. Good weather, excellent swimmer.
Drug-dependency program.
Lost fed. funding.

## Orenberg
Electrocuted while giving ECT.
Shrink. New approach to therapy of depression.
NIH investigation for possible fraudulent reporting of research results.

## Davis
MI.
Headed cancer research institute.
Lost $6 million grant support from Nat'l Cancer Inst. About to lay off three research teams.

## Wicks
Ulcerative colitis → toxic megacolon → peritonitis.
Director of stress-reduction clinic.
Lost 5-year contract w. Cigna for corporate training.

## Carruthers
Stroke.
Headed new hospital based HMO.
Scheduled to break even after 30 months. Lost $20 million between mos. 36–48. Directors likely to dissolve operation.

## Garelli
Duod. ulcer → milk-alkali syndrome → hypercalcemia.
Prof. microbiology. "Sideline" as pres. of venture capital gene-splicing company.
Lost patent fight for rights to recombinant growth hormone.

About to file for bankruptcy.

**Levy**
 MI.
 Vice-chancellor.
 Indictment pending by EPA for illegal dumping of haz-
  ardous waste.

**Loaming**
 Alcoholic hepatitis.
 Head of obesity clinic.
 Malpractice suit for unlawful death of 8 patients.

**Rus**
 Brain tumor.
 Radiologist.
 ?

**Thompson**
 MI.
 Director of renal physiol inst.
 Institute directors insisted on career shift to molecular
  biology.

Montana talked while she read. "Every one of them was
in deep weeds. Six had lost their funding; Levy was going
to be indicted; Loaming was certain to be shut down because of those deaths on his fat farm; Orenberg was
being investigated for fraud; and Thompson was being
pushed into a new area of research that everyone I could
find says he didn't understand. Three died in accidents
that were either thinly disguised suicides or willfully neg-
ligent behavior. Every one of those deaths of 'natural
causes' is a natural result of high stress, except for Rus.
His colleagues say he was happy as a clam. I think he's
the one who would've died anyway."

It was Molly's turn to be skeptical, mostly because she
still was holding out for the Mafia, or Russians. "Life's

tough for everybody at teaching hospitals. Why should these guys be the ones to drop dead and/or kick the bucket?"

"Because they were worse off. Every academic hospital the size of UHOP has rainy-day reserve funds to draw on when their income falls. They can make it through three or four years of poor reimbursements and they can float investigators whose research projects go unfunded for a cycle. UHOP is practically new and is mortgaged to the hilt. The administrators are under phenomenal pressure to save a buck—witness poor old Levy sending biohazard trash to that unlicensed hauler to save one hundred and fifty thousand dollars a year. It blew up in his face when syringes and tubes of blood started washing up on the Jersey shore. The researchers work on a high wire without a safety net. And a lot of patient-care activities like the drug program operated on soft money—you know, their support comes from government grants. And so on. Pull a string and a lifetime's work starts to unravel."

"What about honeys stashed away in expensive condos, or blackmail?" Molly would leave no lurid explanation unexplored.

"Bella knows about these things and says they were clean on the first score. Can't be certain of the second, but I say, who needs it, when it all fits into a neat little package?" Montana scooped the cards together and filed them and their ragged forebears in the recipe box, behind Molly's collection of originals. He snapped the lid shut. "Case closed, my dear."

"Do you think all this is true?" Molly asked.

"Might be. Sounds pretty good when you say it fast."

"Is there any precedent for this?"

"Beats me."

"Maybe you should run this idea by one of your stress-management friends to see if it holds water."

"I just had one of the great ideas of all time, and you want me to talk to a guidance counselor?"

"What would we do about this if you're right?"

"Nothing we can do, as far as I can see. We can't fix the economics of medical care. I'm not sure there's anyone who wants to hear that life's tough. They already know that. Well, maybe some counseling *could* help." He was blabbering. Molly knew that once he started talking about patently unrealistic ideas such as counseling professors, the only way to snap him out of it was to change the subject.

"Back to Epps. How does he fit in?" That brought him back to earth. He didn't even suspect what had happened.

"He doesn't. Nothing in the profile fits. He was a terrific success up to the end. Not a cloud on the horizon. And he couldn't have acquired AIDS by worrying or driving his car too fast. You ought to retire his card. It was a mistake for them to send the thing."

"How do you explain it then?"

"I don't and you shouldn't. I'm sure there's a perfectly reasonable explanation, and it's none of our business."

On the next day, Montana was surprised to find himself part of an old-boy network. His onetime college roommate, Albert Edwards, called to renew a friendship that had lain dormant for twelve years. For old times' sake, they met on the squash courts under the football field where they had played their last game of squash. It had nearly been Bert's last game of anything, since he had caught a squash ball in the eye and had spent ten days in the hospital with both eyes patched, while his doctors gave pessimistic projections about the chances for saving the sight in that eye. During the period of enforced introspection, Bert decided to forsake his plan to become a journalist and to devote himself instead to making money. He had enjoyed a brief lucrative career as a securities analyst. So much so that he was able to retire in his early thirties and could afford to write about things that interested him. Initially, he wrote about the insurance industry, but he had gradually branched out into background articles and books on people and events in the business community.

Bert dressed for the occasion in a scarlet silk eye-patch that diverted attention from his sallow skin and receding hairline. The two picked up exactly where their last conversation had left off. Unfortunately, neither of them could remember the name of Miss October 1968, and they decided she probably wouldn't be worth looking up by this time, anyway. They made their way to a family-run Greek restaurant and sat at a table with a red and white checked oilcloth. Bert had a black Russian and Montana ouzo. While Montana watched his drink whiten with the melting ice, Bert raised the subject of Epps.

"I'm writing a biography of Epps. It's already made its first million, counting rights for prepublication excerpts, serialization, softcover, and the flicks. I've put in a ton of time researching the AIDS angle, but I'm hoping you can push me over the top. Let me tell you a few things about Mr. Squeaky Clean.

"Epps had a more interesting past than he let on during the last thirty-five years. At college, he apparently hosted very exclusive private parties that included a variety of exotic entertainment. Some of these included audience participation. He also had a *very* close friendship with a fellow undergraduate.

"My problem is this. I can't find any whiff of anything illegal, immoral, or fattening since then. And I've looked in all the right places and talked to everybody who should know. So, my good friend, can you tell me please if it is possible that he could have acquired his ultimately fatal infection during a college fling?"

Montana swirled his iceless opalescent ouzo in its glass. "You've spent weeks researching death by AIDS and you have to ask whether the infection was around decades ago? You can't be so great a ninny not to know the answer to that one."

"Right again, Mountain Man. What I really want to know is whether there's any gold in the blood transfusion that the dear departed received. I do know that folks get it that way, and that there wasn't as much talk about his as we pencil pushers might have liked. How come?"

"Maybe there wasn't anything to say. It might help you to know that you can't get AIDS from your own blood. Are you going to keep drinking that sweet stuff?"

Bert ordered another round. He raised his glass and offered a toast, "To my fine feathered informant. I christen thee 'Sore Throat.'"

"Most people think I'm a pain in a different part of the anatomy. Now, I have a question for you. What would you think if I told you that a large handful of my hospital's distinguished faculty have died either in suspicious accidents or from various organs exploding?"

"'Organs exploding'! You mean like they swallowed dynamite?" Edwards was a stickler for detail.

"Almost. Listen carefully. People who were losing their source of funds, or who falsified research data, or who were going to be indicted for professional misadventures, or who watched the free-enterprise system deny them the fortune they believed was theirs dropped dead when their hearts stopped, the blood vessels in their brains burst, their livers were pickled in alcohol, their intestines perforated, they drove into oncoming traffic, drowned during an afternoon swim, or stuck their fingers into an electric socket."

"'Electric socket'?" Bert's eye narrowed suspiciously.

"An electrode he knew better than to handle. Same difference."

94

"I would say that your colleagues were suffering from the executive-stress syndrome."

"You mean you've heard of it?"

"Everybody has. We invented it, but like much that's made America great, the Japanese perfected it. Highly successful executives are so grimly focused on their goals that they can't cope with failure, even though they're still working full tilt. Usually, they keep working harder and harder until they drop. Or they cut corners. Sometimes, recognizing failure, they bail out in the only way they see as honorable. It was a terrific problem when the yen doubled its value against the dollar. A lot of the major Japanese corporations lost their CEOs during the next year."

It was Montana's turn to narrow his eyes. "Did you just make that up?"

"Of course not. It's part of mainstream American culture. *Time* did a piece on Messrs. Nakamura, Kondo, Ohno, and Hattori, who ran large companies in Japan until they died in much the way you describe. If you took your nose out of your professional journals once in a while, you'd know all about it."

They turned their attention to supper. Montana had marinated octopus, followed by squid. Bert had lamb's eyes and another black Russian. They passed up the invitation to join in the dancing, contenting themselves with breaking plates and buying drinks for the participants. Two liters of retsina later, they helped put the chairs on the tables, sweep the floor, and put out the cat. Outside, Bert gave Montana a small gift-wrapped box.

"A memento I've been meaning to pass along to you. Keep it around as a good luck charm. Give my love to Molly. I'll look you both up when I get back to town." Since his last trip to town had been twelve years before, this was not a promise to be taken seriously.

Bert headed for Thirtieth Street Station to catch the 2 A.M. train to New York. Montana accompanied him to

**95**

Twentieth Street, then turned off toward home. He made it into the house, up two flights of stairs, and into the bathroom before Whimsy figured out that they had been invaded. He tried to hide his embarrassment by burying his face between Montana's knees and wagging his tail in a blur. Between pats, Montana opened the box. It contained a lacquered ebony stand affixed to which was a squash ball decorated as an eye. The inscription on the base read "Here's looking at you, kid."

# EIGHTEEN

THE MONTANAS really and truly gave up the pursuit of the Epps affair—for about two days, until Montana received a letter from Grace Epps asking whether he would grant her the kindness of a meeting. The simple unadorned handwriting in dark-gray ink on pale-gray stationery evoked her well-known public persona. An important figure in her own right, Grace Epps was a product of the same social stratum as her late husband. Independently wealthy, she had established a career in charitable activities before marrying Epps at the age of thirty-six. As respectable, Republican, and rich as she was, she was an extremely effective feminist of long standing. She invested her money in women—including women's colleges and graduate schools, galleries, orchestras, and publishing houses that supported women.

Hundreds of successful women in all sorts of careers owed part of their success to Grace's good works. Even Carola benefited from a Grace Epps program that provided an interest-free loan so that she could buy her two-hundred-year-old cello.

The Epps's marriage had been wildly successful through its entire twenty-plus years. While raising two picture-perfect children, Grace had continued her own activities and had taken on a number of additional ones that rounded out her husband's. Grace also had the personal gift of putting everyone she met at ease. After a few minutes in her presence, headaches vanished, ulcers stopped grumbling, and low back pain became a distant memory. Her admirers claimed she could make the blind see, the dumb speak, and the lame walk. She had no detractors.

Montana went to the Epps's estate the next day. He drove up the half-mile-long private road to the main house at the top of the circular drive and was met by a blond linebacker wearing a freshly laundered pair of Calvins and a hooded navy sweatshirt with EPPS in half-inch red letters where the alligator usually lives. He took Montana's keys to move the Civic a decent distance from the house, and told him just to ring the bell. Hearing no tone when he pressed same, Montana had the uneasy feeling of not knowing whether he'd pushed the button hard enough and wondered when it would be time to try again. As he contemplated this strategic problem, the massive mahogany door opened and he was face-to-face with a white-haired woman in the Katharine Hepburn mold.

"Dr. Montana, please come in." She had a firm comfortable handshake, and led him to a cozy cream-colored parlor off the main hallway. They sat facing each other in soft velvet armchairs. She poured tea. "Thanks so much for making time to see me, Dr. Montana. Dan Belkins suggested I speak to you. I don't care what the world thinks, but I owe it to Van to find the truth. The hospital assures me the blood transfusion wasn't the cause of his illness. Is there anything else you can tell me?"

"I was really only a spectator, Mrs. Epps. I did look at the transfusion records. There shouldn't have been any HIV-positive units of blood in the bank in the first place, and even if there was an antibody-negative, virus-infected unit, I don't think there's any chance your husband could have received any blood except his own. It does seem clear that your husband probably became infected sometime after his surgery."

"How do you know that?"

"When he donated his blood, it was tested for HIV antibody, just like every other unit of blood that the blood bank collects. Since the test was negative, it's unlikely, but not impossible, that he acquired his infection more than a month or two before then."

"Doctor, I am quite sure my husband did not have liaisons or habits that would have exposed him to AIDS. I'm convinced something happened that neither you nor I know about. I need your help to discover what it was."

Montana began to say something noncommittal but was cut off in mid "well, uhh."

"I appreciate your tact, Doctor Montana. I realize that spouses are invariably wrong in this matter and you have no reason to share my faith. I know that I knew Van too well to have been deceived about this, but I'll put this to you as a medical problem. What is the usual incubation period for AIDS?"

"It's usually a few years."

"And you say he acquired his infection no earlier than last year."

"Yes."

"Does it ever have a shorter incubation period?"

"It tends to be shorter when there's intense exposure."

"For example?"

Montana had been thrown, pinned, and counted out before he realized there was a wrestling match. He had been an expert witness in a variety of court cases, but he'd never been led so directly and with so little apparent effort to a conclusion that supported the opposing side. She was right out of *Adam's Rib*.

"You're quite right, Mrs. Epps, the incubation period is shortest after a contaminated transfusion. This would be about the right time for him to develop symptoms if his transfusion was the cause. You knew that, didn't you?"

"Please call me Grace. Yes, I did, but it really only supported what I suspected all along. Now, is Dr. Larraby's suggestion about getting infected in the research lab plausible?"

"No."

"Why does he insist on telling it to me, then? I'm not the penny press. He can't really believe I'd think differently of Van because of a specious claim like that. Does he believe it?"

"He shouldn't, but he might. It's probably easier for him to use that explanation than to ponder the alternatives. All of the others are bad for someone."

"I should say so," Grace said with emphasis. "To get back to my request. I believe more strongly than anything that Van could only have gotten AIDS from his transfusion. I hope I've at least made you keep that possibility alive in your own mind. Other than you, there is no one else in a position to look into this."

"Actually the best person for this job is Dr. Low, the blood bank director."

"My dear man," she gently responded, "Rudolph Low is the last person in the world to tackle this question. A fine man, a decent man—but he couldn't find an outhouse in a heat wave. And if Perrin Larraby doesn't want to think about the blood bank's making a mistake, then the man who runs the department for him surely isn't going to help him reconsider. Dan Belkins assures me you really are the only one who can do it."

"All right, Mrs. Epps, I honestly don't think there will be anything there, but I'll go back over the records. It might take a while. I'll keep you posted."

"Thank you so much. Let me know if there's anything you need. The Epps foundation is quite efficient at providing discreet help to all manner of people."

As Montana drove back along the Main Line, he remembered that Molly used to say Epps reminded her of Spencer Tracy. Grace Epps was a remarkable and fascinating woman, and his ego was feeling no pain. Professional doubter though he was, he had agreed to go back over the transfusion story because she made him believe she really would have known if Epps had come by his infection in the "usual" way. Her impeccable logic about the incubation period was secondary for him as well as for her, although it was remarkable for a layperson to assemble the pieces as she had.

The problem was that he hadn't the faintest idea how to proceed. He'd already looked at the blood bank's records, interviewed both the boss and the hired help, and all their pins were in a perfect row. He surely wasn't going to discover another transfusion during an African safari. And the whole premise of his poking around was that there wasn't a lover tucked away in Omaha, far from the probing eyes of the press.

# NINETEEN

MONTANA MADE it home well after the witching hour, nine o'clock. Molly pulled the blanket over her head and mumbled, "Five more minutes." Montana slid into bed, put his arms around her, and settled in for a good snuggle, maybe more, depending. He whispered in her ear, "She's much cuter than she looks in the paper." No response. "She says he was clean as a whistle." Still nothing. "She thinks the blood bank pulled the old switcheroo." Action.

"How come?"

"She says she knew her man and he couldn't have done her wrong."

"And?"

"And she points out he was antibody-negative when he donated before his surgery, and that the incubation period was too short for him to have gotten sick if he was infected afterward, unless he got a big hit, such as from a contaminated transfusion."

"This calls for a snack."

Armies and athletes traveled on their stomachs, Montana had once heard. He didn't know about armies, but he could vouch for the latter. Molly wriggled into a T-shirt and led the way to the kitchen. From behind yesterday's leftovers, and the day before's leftovers, and something of unknown vintage, she extracted a fresh napoleon.

"How did that get into the back of the refrigerator?"

"It must have gotten lost on its way to my stomach. What are you going to do about Epps?"

"Beats me. I can go back to the blood bank, but there really isn't anything else there to find. I wonder whether it's worth digging for his old medical record. It was lost when I looked before."

Molly was carving out the cream filling with her tongue. "I've yet to meet a medical record that said anything useful. Dan Belkins is his regular doc, right?"

"Yeah."

"Why don't you talk to him? Maybe he has some records in his office."

"He's the one who told Grace Epps to call me. I'm sure he'd have said so by now if he knew anything interesting."

"You mean she said he told her to call. Anyway, if it doesn't wheeze or cough up phlegm, a pulmonary guy probably wouldn't know it's interesting. You don't have a lot of choices, dear. It's him or the blood bank. I'd see him first and then go see if you can ask the wonderful computer how it could have messed up. Back to bed." Napoleon's ghost lingered on, a creamy wisp on the tip of her nose.

"Where did you get an Amherst T-shirt?"

"I won it off some guy."

Montana groaned. It seemed every new rower on the river ended up contributing to Molly's wardrobe. Invariably, a six-foot sculler would find himself proposing a match race against this amiable, well-proportioned, but decidedly nonmuscular woman resting on her oars, who allowed how maybe he could get a little more out of his glide. "Someday, one of these chumps is going to win, and there's going to be a mighty big fuss when you have to hand over your shirt on the spot."

"Could be," she allowed, heading for bed. "Maybe you can help me practice getting it off with my modesty intact. Are you coming?"

# TWENTY

MONTANA made several attempts the next day before he found Belkins without a crowd around. Belkins confirmed Grace Epps's story and said there really wasn't anything in his records that could be of the remotest use, but that Montana was welcome to come and look. That afternoon Montana sat in a spare examining room in Belkins's office, where he read and reread the chart.

Epps had been just about as healthy as advertised. Ten years of medical records filled only eighteen pages, most of which were lab test results. He had had mild asthma since childhood and about one minor illness per year. The hip surgery was treatment for an old college football injury.

What wasn't so ordinary, at least in retrospect, was an illness that began about three weeks after his hip surgery. Epps had complained of fever, a severe headache, generalized aching, and a sore neck. Belkins had made a house call, thereby confirming the gulf between the rich and the very rich. His examination of Epps revealed swollen glands and a mild stiff neck. He thought seriously about doing a lumbar puncture to look for bacterial meningitis, but figured Epps looked too good for him to have that. His impression was "probable viral illness," for which he prescribed aspirin and watched his patient like a hawk, in the event he should stop looking too good to have bacterial meningitis. The episode resolved over ten days without specific diagnosis or therapy.

Montana caught Belkins at the end of his office hours and showed him the note. "Dan, could this have been acute HIV infection?"

Belkins stared at the ceiling. "You know, I'm sure I never considered it. And I still wouldn't. I see hundreds of people with those syndromes. If I looked for HIV in all of them, I'd scare half of Chestnut Hill out of its mind."

"You're right. You wouldn't consider it and they shouldn't. But I bet you would if your next patient told you he was just back from a business trip to San Francisco and had spent an evening cruising the bars in the Castro." The epidemiologist in Montana was clamoring to explain that this was yet another everyday application of Bayesian inference. Your certainty that a man with a nondescript illness had acute symptomatic HIV infection depended both on how likely you believed him to have been exposed to the virus and on the nature of the illness itself. It also helped to know that HIV had belatedly been recognized to infect nerve cells and to cause both acute and chronic neurologic symptoms. Aseptic meningitis, which Epps appeared to have had, was one of the symptoms. Montana the clinician managed to keep Montana the epidemiologist under wraps.

"We know for sure Epps was infected. We've been dancing around trying to figure out when it happened and here's a neon sign pointing to his hospitalization last year. Any other suggestions?"

"I suggest you not mention this to the L's."

"Who?"

"Larraby, Low, or the Lawyers. They aren't going to appreciate your digging up iffy evidence that their system broke down and killed one of the most famous men in the world. If you can't do better, you should keep it to yourself. If you can, you might still want to keep it to yourself."

Montana pondered that advice while he sat in traffic, heading back to UHOP. That illness wasn't proof, but it did greatly strengthen his concern that Epps had been infected at the hospital. It was perfectly clear to Montana that he hadn't gotten it by walking down the hall or sitting next to a patient with AIDS or even by sharing the infamous toilet seat. Since infection in the hospital was the best bet, the answer had to be in the blood. Belkins was probably right about Larraby et al.'s not being enthusiastic about Montana's raising the possibility. On the other hand, he really couldn't ignore it now. If the hospital had screwed up one certified clean transfusion, it could do it to others. It might already have done it to others. Other hospitals might be doing it. The tabloids might have been right all along. The public's health might be at stake. Low, as director of the blood bank, would certainly want to know about this. Larraby probably didn't need to know until Montana and Low had taken it further.

Montana called Low at the blood bank. He was directed to the coffee shop, where he found Low with two crullers and hot chocolate. He told him about Epps's postop illness and his new concern.

"Like I told you, Montana, there isn't any way on earth we could have released the wrong unit of blood. You know safety comes first in my shop. The system's airtight. There's no room for human error. The computer runs it and it doesn't make mistakes. He might have gotten infected here, but it wasn't his blood."

"There's really no way the system could have broken down?"

"No; that's three times I've told you and the answer won't change. Give the transfusion business a rest. The Red Cross, the Joint Commission, and the American Association of Blood Banks say we do a fine job. My God, I gave my own mother blood with this system. If you're convinced he was exposed here, go chat up your friends in anesthesia. They probably reused some needles to save a buck."

"I'll check with them. Meanwhile, can I come by for a demonstration of the ID and tracking system on your computer? I'd like to see exactly how it works."

The powdered sugar was flying off Low's upper lip, making it look like he was breathing smoke. "The girls won't have time to show you. I'll be pretty busy for the next few weeks. I'm getting ready to go to the Blood Bank meetings in New Orleans. I'll give you a call when I get back."

Shoulders turn cold with appalling speed, Montana realized as he watched Low's massive frame plow through the maze of tables and then turn toward the cafeteria. Montana went back to his office, called the blood bank and asked when Lorraine—the tech who had shown him how to use the computer—would be on duty again. She was spending the month taking blood from donors.

Montana realized he was overdue to donate. He was usually overdue to donate, since, in deference to Molly's wardrobe, he waited until they were giving out free sweatshirts to donors. This happened only once a year, and he was damned if he was going to donate for a beach ball or a greaseball sandwich at the cafeteria. This once, though, he figured he could accept a coffee cup in the name of a good cause. He could tell Molly he'd won it from a phlebotomist.

Trekking back double time, to be able to donate during Low's lunch, he signed the customary affidavit that he was of good character, didn't have malaria, hadn't slept with any guys since 1977, weighed more than ninety pounds, and promised to eat a good dinner. Disaster struck immediately after he was shown to the reclining

**106**

chair. No Lorraine. Barbara. Although Montana eschewed stereotypes, her platinum blond beehive and bubble gum seemed to be omens. Bad ones.

"I thought Lorraine was in the donor room these days."

"She's at lunch. I'm covering."

A medium-sized pink bubble appeared and then was slowly engulfed by her frosted pink lips. Montana watched in horror as she swabbed his forearm with antiseptic, then used her (nonsterile) frosted pink-nailed finger to search out a vein. With a mighty heave, she pushed the fourteen-gauge needle that resembled a small pipe through his skin, through the vein, and into the tendon sheath below. Waves of nausea swept over him.

"Geez, I guess I'll have to try the other side."

Beads of sweat glistened on Montana's forehead and on the rest of him as she repeated the ritual on his other arm. This time, the needle came to rest in a vein and blood started to collect in the plastic bag hanging from the arm of the chair.

"How do you make those labels on the bag?"

"I dunno, the computer makes them."

"Don't you get the computer to make them?"

"Well, actually I have a lot of trouble with it, so one of the other girls does it for me. Computers were always a problem for me. You know, this blood's running awful slow. Maybe you could squeeze on this ball."

"Do you use the computer when you hand out the blood?"

"Oh yeah, that's a snap. You just put the card with the patient's name in the reader, push the red button, and wave the pointer over the label on the bag of blood. Just like at the market. The computer screen says: 'This blood is okay. Thank you, Barbara.' Then it gives you labels that you stick on the blood and the card. You know, that bag just isn't filling up. It doesn't seem to be my day. Do you want me to try a different vein?"

Montana allowed as how he had to get back to work and promised to return. He departed the blood bank with compression bandages over the gaping wounds on his arms and headed for the pharmacy to get some Tylenol. He briefly considered the possibility that Low had foreseen his foray and had laid this trap specially for him (a Low blow, he thought through the pain). This line of reasoning was interrupted by a janitor who pointed out to him that he was leaving a trail of red drops along the corridor. Montana thanked him, though he wasn't sure whose welfare the man was looking out for, and changed course for the emergency room, where he booked himself in as a trauma case. He'd paid a substantial price but had learned at least that the distribution side of the blood-matching process really was idiotproof. If he had only remembered to pick up his mug.

# TWENTY-ONE

AT TIMES like this, when he had suffered a setback and was in pain to boot, Montana forced himself to remember that he was among the most fortunate of men. He was happily married, had wonderful children, and had been to a Richard and Mimi Farina concert. And he was lucky enough to find Bella at her desk when he got back to his office.

"You look as though you just auditioned for the lead part in the spring pageant about the Resurrection," she remarked, looking at the darkening stains on his sleeves. "I wouldn't go to the dress rehearsal if I were you."

"I just met a blood bank tech named Barbara."

An enormous smile spread across her face. "She's a double *O* tech, licensed to kill. Sweet as can be, though."

"I was hoping to find Lorraine. Do you know her?" Stupid question.

"Sure, are you sweet on her?" High school romance was never far from her mind. She had started to make real use of the hospital's computer system only when she discovered it knew all the physicians' ages and marital status. She had used the system to establish a quiet but eminently effective dating service. Her modus operandi was to run a general check of all new house officers soon after the influx every July. Since the computer kept a record of people who accessed files like these that contained sensitive information, she covered her tracks by using the head micro lab tech's password. This subterfuge was a source of considerable amusement to those who knew, since the head tech was among the least likely people in the world to go after such information. Bella had begun this life of petty crime mostly as revenge, after discovering that her own computer profile would give the date of her last period to anyone who asked. Never mind that it was leftover information from when she delivered her youngest at Women's, twelve years before. Montana drew two morals from this. He never ever told his password to anyone, and he never made Bella angry.

"I'd like to know more about what was going on in the blood bank last year when Epps got his transfusion. She told me she was around then."

"What do you want to know?"

"If she remembers how they were handling blood then. And if there was anything special about Epps's blood. She told me she remembers when he donated it, so she might have paid attention. And anything else you can think of. This is mostly a wild-goose chase and Dr. Low is already pissed off at me, so I'd rather not make a big deal of this."

"You know, I bet Lorraine'd like to check out the happy hour at the Vermilion Border. I'll give her a ring."

Confident that his problem was in good hands, Montana started to poke at a great pile of papers having to do with the hospital's nascent postdischarge surveillance program. This albatross had started as a consummately simple idea. Since many infections that people picked up in the hospital didn't show up until after they left, it was impossible to tell just how many there were. The problem was getting bigger as hospital stays shortened in the face of cost-containment pressures. Montana's idea was to send a questionnaire to patients after they had been home for a while, asking them about any problems they'd had since their discharge.

Working out the mechanics of getting these questionnaires into the hands of the patients and back to the Epidemiology Unit took forever. Montana's friends in administration thought the way to handle it was to give each patient a self-addressed postcard on the way out the door. Having gone out the door himself once or twice, Montana knew most of the cards wouldn't survive the ride home, and the rest would certainly be mislaid. Six months went into designing a full-page form that folded up to show the patient's address on the outside, and that then could be refolded by the patient to show the hospital's address for the return trip. Getting the patients' names onto the questionnaires required another eight months. Each week, the hospital's mainframe computer made a tape containing the name, rank, serial number, and other important information about the patients who had been discharged. The little computer in his unit read these tapes, waited two weeks, and then printed mailing

**110**

labels from those records. But first, it had to figure out which patients had died—families hated to get notes from the hospital asking how the departed was doing. And someone had to tell it which babies had been put up for adoption. Grandparents took exception to learning of their new status via a note inquiring about the infant. All this was no mean feat when you were dealing with sixty five thousand admissions per year. After they had produced their first batch of questionnaires, it took another three months to figure out the post office's bulk-mailing rules for nonprofit institutions. Montana now knew more about three-digit zip code sorts than the postmaster general.

The system was on the verge of producing terrific information. The tapes came; the computer sent out the mail to the right folks; it waited for replies; it sent out reminders after three weeks to patients who hadn't been heard from; it printed telephone numbers of patients who didn't answer the reminder; and it recorded responses.

Which was a tribute to Selma Sloane, a nurse turned programmer who consulted for Montana. After UHOP's Management Information Systems group washed its hands of the project, she designed the system from the ground up. She got the MIS boys to tell her how their own computer files were organized, wrote the specifications for information transfer, fiddled all the pieces to make one computer talk to another, and wrote all of the software that made the system fly.

The system had already distinguished itself. The best feature proved to be an add-on question inviting patients to comment on their hospitalization. About half did, and three-quarters of those said what a wonderful place UHOP was and how they would certainly come back the next time they needed to have their gallbladders out. The remainder pointed out the kind of thing every hospital administrator needed to know. Were it not for the questionnaires, the sadist would still be working the night shift on the fourth floor and ladies with two broken arms would still be dining doggie style.

In addition, every doc received a list of his or her patients' infections every month. They were so pleased. What Montana and Selma were working on now was denominators. Instead of just forwarding the problem responses back to the docs, Montana wanted to give them a panoramic view of what had happened to all of UHOP's patients. That way, you'd know whether your six infections a year were unfortunate or really bad news. Pulling it off properly was going to tax both Montana and the remarkable Ms. Sloane. They would need to know not only who the patients were and whether they lived but why they were hospitalized, and what type of surgery they had, and how long the surgery took, and a variety of other things that affected their chance of getting infected. UHOP was already laboring under the burden of unwisely used statistics. For example, the State Department of Public Health required hospitals to post their cesarean section rate. Without adjusting the rate for the number of high-risk deliveries (UHOP did a ton of them), the figure was phenomenally misleading. Montana's effort to avoid similar problems had already eaten up several months and he was nowhere near the end. Selma remained sanguine, however. She said as long as UHOP didn't cut off the electricity, they could do it. She didn't say when.

On the other hand, identifying risk factors was an adventure of its own. On clear days, it seemed they might even figure out a way to prevent the infections instead of predicting them. This wasn't one of those days. Montana took the stuff home with him. At least Isaac would enjoy playing with his programmable calculator.

# TWENTY-TWO

THE NEXT morning, Bella arrived at work shortly before noon. She looked terrible.

"Do you have any idea how much that woman can drink? Never again, boss or no boss," she said, elbows on her desk, hands holding her head as though it were tomorrow's pathology exhibit.

Something like this happened approximately twice a year. Montana started a fresh pot of coffee, fetched the ice bag from the filing cabinet, and went back to working on the questionnaire data while the extremes of temperature worked their magic on her. Twenty minutes later, she rejoined the living.

"Lorraine sends her regrets about yesterday. They were shorthanded and couldn't pay as much attention as usual to Barbara. Lorraine was pleased as could be to talk about Mr. Epps. He was the only subject of conversation in the blood bank for weeks after the news got out about his having AIDS. The girls went back and checked the record from the blood he donated. It was fine, just like you'd expect. They were sort of surprised, though, that Dr. Low didn't want to see it.

"They think they handled blood then just like they do now. One person keeps track of the HIV-antibody-positive blood. Last year it was Adrienne Martinson. She left about a year ago to be head tech at the Red Cross regional blood bank in Connecticut. She lives in Hartford. Here's her telephone number. I'm still feeling terrible. I better take this as a sick day. I'll get Carola to cover my floors. If my mother calls, tell her I'll pick up the kids at six. Thank her for keeping them last night. See you tomorrow."

Montana hoped Bella never decided to investigate the CIA. The only question was which would go first, the national defense plans or her liver. He called Hartford to discover Adrienne was on vacation, visiting her brother in Cape May. Montana prayed that, married or no, Adrienne was using her maiden name. He found her at the third Martinson in the Cape May County listing and explained he was wrapping up a few details for UHOP so it could close out its documentation before the next accreditation visit. She was extremely cordial and had been planning to go to Center City anyway to see the girls in the blood bank, so she'd stop by his office after that. Which, to his surprise, she did that same afternoon.

"I really appreciate your coming, Ms. Martinson. I'm stuck with the job of filling in the records of how we handled HIV-antibody-positive blood since the beginning of the testing program. I know the official procedure hasn't changed since then, but I need to hear how it was actually done. The ladies there told me you'd be the best person to talk to."

"You mean Lorraine said I might know something about Mr. Epps's transfusion."

He held his hand up to the X-ray viewbox on the wall. "Am I that transparent?"

"No, but Lorraine is. Which do you want to talk about first?"

This woman ought to be in Epidemiology, thought Montana. "The protocols, please."

"We started screening all donor units for HIV antibody in the spring of 1985. For the first eight or nine months, we only had a few positive units and we saved them for Dr. Zenana at Penn. He was collecting infected blood from all over the country, looking for variant strains of the virus. Blood for him got a special orange Day-Glo label, RESEARCH ONLY, and was kept on the top shelf of the big refrigerator. We'd call his lab and Dr. Zenana usually came by himself on Sunday evening to collect it. The donor's name went on a special deferral list so we wouldn't take any more of his blood. Dr. Low was supposed to tell the donor the results and discuss the implications. But he was so uncomfortable about counseling that I'm not sure he always did."

"Who knew about the deferral list?"

"Everybody knew about it, but Dr. Low had the only copy. There wasn't any need since the computer knew all of the deferrals and wouldn't let us take blood from those people if they tried to donate again. When you typed in their name, the computer wouldn't let you go on if the person had been notified. It was supposed to keep the reason confidential, and so it didn't tell you why the person couldn't donate. If the person didn't know yet, it would let you take the blood, so you wouldn't have to be the one to tell him, but it put an orange research label on it automatically. Dr. Low was very proud of the way it worked. It was the only system of its kind anywhere at the time. A bunch of bigwigs came through to inspect the system, to see if other hospitals could use it. Dr. Larraby and some reporters even came, too.

"While I was here, that system never really got put to the test, though. There weren't many positives, so we all basically knew who they were; I don't remember any of them coming back to donate again. I guess they heard from Dr. Low or got tested someplace else and found out that way."

"Did you have any positive units around the time that Mr. Epps donated his blood?"

"When was that?"

"A year ago, May."

"No, we only had one positive in April last year and the next one was in June. Actually, I remember we were keeping a unit for Dr. Zenana when I crossmatched Mr. Epps's blood before his surgery."

"Is there any way those units could have been mixed up?"

"No. The labels are very clear and even if you made a mistake, the computer would catch it when you ran it through the scanner before you handed it out."

"Could the labels have been reversed?"

"I don't see how. They're put on when the blood is collected and the units were collected at different times."

"Could the labels have fallen off somehow and been swapped?"

"The labels are plastic-coated with adhesive on the back, you know. You'd have to pull them off and they wouldn't stick a second time; it couldn't just happen."

"Whose blood was it?"

"Was what?"

"Was HIV-antibody-positive."

"You know that's confidential. Nobody is supposed to know."

"Everybody and her sister in the blood bank knew. And I bet their boyfriends and their uncles knew. Tell you what. The Epidemiology Unit knows about all of the known HIV-positive patients who are admitted. Has he been hospitalized since then?"

"Yes. I guess it's all right, then. His name was Evans Rice."

Montana knew Rice, an extremely likable and articulate architect. Montana had been consulted when Rice was admitted for intractable diarrhea, which clinched the diagnosis of AIDS. The problem turned out to be cryptosporidiosis, a parasitic infection peculiar to men and women with AIDS and normal day-care workers. Early in his illness, they had talked about Rice rehabilitating the Montanas' kitchen. But there wasn't any cure for the diarrhea and the man had gone down from 160 pounds to 115 in the ensuing two months. Montana hadn't heard from him since he left the hospital but was pretty sure he was no longer alive.

"Well, it sounds like a pretty snappy system. Have any other blood banks adopted it?"

"Quite a few, actually. The computer system is the most important thing Dr. Low's done. We were all really pleased for him, because he was always worried that he'd lose his job because he didn't do any research or publish anything."

"I'm questioned out. I'm glad you were visiting. Do you like Connecticut?"

"Actually, it's not working out too well. My boyfriend had been planning to open a Thai restaurant in Lower Merion. He moved up with me, but everybody there eats Polynesian sweet and sour. I thought that might be a problem, so I told them at work I'd try it for a while. I'll probably come back home."

"What made you decide to go?"

"Dr. Low asked if I was interested. The Connecticut Red Cross wanted to introduce our system to its affiliated banks and he told them it would be easier if they had an experienced person to demonstrate it. He told me I could come back after a year or two if I didn't like it."

"You've been a real help, I hope you come back soon. Please let me know when you get back. I love green curry."

"Thanks, Dr. Montana. I will. I have to go. Lorraine's taking me to a new place for Happy Hour. She wants to cash in a free drink coupon they gave her yesterday."

# TWENTY-THREE

"YOU WERE one for two, and I'm stuck." Montana was inspecting his empty teacup, trying to decide whether it was due for its bimonthly washing. He told the kids that the patina of past teas improved the bouquet. They said the cup was gross.

"Which one?" Molly was watching TV.

"Epps developed aseptic meningitis and adenopathy a few weeks after his hip was fixed. It can't not have been the opening round of his HIV infection. So he almost for sure got infected in the hospital, and blood's the only way to go. I came up empty in the blood bank, though."

"Really nothing at all?"

"Not unless you call a foolproof system for keeping track of blood something." He told her the substance of his interview with Adrienne. As he spoke, she paid less and less attention to her program. About halfway through, she turned it off, an unprecedented occurrence.

"If it shoots bullets and smokes, maybe it's a gun." Molly talked like David Addison when she watched "Moonlighting." Montana gave her a blank look. "Have I married the last of the innocents? You've figured out that he must have gotten a bad transfusion, and that there was a unit of infected blood sitting around in the refrigerator, and that the units couldn't have been switched accidentally, and that the tech who knew about it got an invitation out of the blue to move three hundred miles away—with a guarantee that she can come home if she doesn't like it, and that doesn't suggest anything to you?"

"It suggests to me that you're going to have to stop reading pulp novels. Guys like Epps don't get murdered. And if you did want to do him in, you wouldn't pick something that might not make him sick at all, and if it did, probably wouldn't have a noticeable effect for years. What kind of stupid, half-crazed killers do you think we let into our blood bank? UHOP has a reputation to protect, you know."

"Aren't you the guy who gives lectures all over the world about letting the facts speak for themselves? These facts are screaming."

"Maybe, but they aren't talking about anything we can follow up on. Low's already not speaking to me. He isn't going to pat me on the back if I tell him somebody purposely screwed up his blood bank and all of its safeguards. The hospital's public-relations office is not likely to schedule a press conference so I can tell the world my wife thinks the man was murdered. And the police are likely to want at least a little proof that a crime was committed. There isn't any way on earth to prove the man got dirty blood."

"Maybe, maybe not. Did I smell chocolate cheesecake in the vicinity of your briefcase?"

"Maybe, maybe not. What do you mean, 'Maybe, maybe not'?"

"First, the mysterious Madame Molly will make a prediction." She pressed her fingers to her eyes and swayed back and forth. She continued in an eastern European accent, "Epps and Rice had compatible major blood-group antigens." Eyebrows raised, she peeked around her fingers, looking for a response from Montana.

He nodded, "Epps was AB and Rice was A. Surprised, aren't you? I remember Epps's from when I checked his transfusion history and I know Rice's because they were looking for donors for him when he was in with diarrhea." He was so pleased with himself.

"Madame Molly is never surprised, even when you know the answer to her questions. Had it been reversed, Epps would have suffered a catastrophe as soon as he received the bogus unit. Fever, chills, renal failure, the works. Now for my next prediction." She put her fingers back over her eyes. "The great Dr. Montana does not know their Rh types."

"And the great Dr. Montana doesn't care, either."

Madame Molly yielded the floor to the hematologist who operated out of the same brain. "It's possible that Epps was missing some blood-group antigen that Rice had. The most likely mismatch would be in their Rh systems. Each of them separately had about a one in seven chance of being Rh-negative. So there's approximately a 12.24 percent chance that Epps was negative and Rice was positive. And if that's the case, then Epps would have made Rh antibody, and there might still have been some antibody in his blood when he fell sick and came back to your venerable institution last month. And I recall your clinical lab keeps old blood samples around almost forever, so there might still be some to be had. There are other antigen systems one could consider, but they cost more than cheesecake."

Montana tossed her his briefcase as he headed for the door. Twenty minutes later, he was knocking at the blood bank's door. Geraldine somebody let him in. "Hi, Dr. Montana, we were talking about you today. Adrienne said you were real nice to her. What are you doing around the hospital this time of night?" Montana explained that he wanted to check the blood types of two donors. "No problem. If you want, I'll show you how so you can do it yourself if you need to look up anything else later on."

She showed him how to access individual donors' rec-

ords. These started with a list of all the person's donations. One then selected specific units and saw the information Low had once described to him. Montana looked
up Rice first. The initial screen showed a flashing notice;
"Permanent deferral—contact blood bank director." The
next screen showed Rice's blood type, A, which Montana
had known, and his Rh type, positive. No surprise there,
since that put him in the 86 percent who were Rh-
positive. Then Montana pulled up the information on
Epps. He had actually seen this screen briefly when Lorraine had helped him look for Epps's donors, but he
hadn't paid much attention to it. Molly be praised, Epps
was Rh-negative. She had filled an inside straight. He offered silent thanks to the computer, and to Low for making it so user-friendly. He gave ordinary thanks to
Geraldine for the lesson, left the hospital, did a buck and
wing in the parking lot, and headed for an all-night pa-
tisserie. He was not one to begrudge a woman "more
than cheesecake" just because her first surmise had
proven to be correct.

# TWENTY-FOUR

MONTANA'S secretary interrupted the next day's meeting. "Dr. Larraby's office called. You're supposed to go
there immediately. They said to be sure you understood
the part about right away."

Carola and Bella were impressed. "Maybe he wants you to go to Washington with him." "I bet there are pigeon droppings in the executive bathroom." "Tell him Bella doesn't have a date this Friday." "Do you think he has a social disease?"

Montana reserved judgment, but on the whole he didn't look forward to unplanned meetings, and especially not this one. He tied his necktie as he made his way to Larraby's office. Larraby and Low were waiting together. Low was somber as could be. No pleasantries. No food in his fist. Larraby was his usual professional self.

"Dr. Montana, would you explain your recent activities to me? Dr. Low tells me you and your underlings have been harassing his staff for weeks, even after he specifically requested you to stop."

"I believe Mr. Epps may have acquired his AIDS through the transfusion he received here last year during his hip surgery. I've been—"

"Dr. Low assures me there is no chance such a thing could have happened."

"There are several things, though, that don't fit in, Dr. Larraby." Montana told him about Epps's acute illness, the absence of any other plausible source of infection, and the presence of a contaminated unit of blood while Epps's blood was in the bank. Low sat and stared at the framed architectural drawing of the cupola above the UHOP main entrance. His well-exercised jaw muscles were locked in trismus.

"Coincidences abound in modern life, Dr. Montana. As our epidemiologist, you have been an eloquent proponent of a reasoned approach to chance events. I recommend you adhere to your own precepts here."

"Dr. Larraby, we need to investigate even the smallest chance that there was a mixup. There are so many safeguards in the system that such an accident would imply a generic defect in the system's software." Montana saw no

122

point in raising Molly's murder hypothesis. Better to blame a poor helpless machine. "We and every other blood bank that's adopted the system might be putting patients at risk of all kinds of mismatches."

Low remained frozen. Larraby reasoned with Montana. "There isn't even the smallest chance, as you put it, of such a problem. You have determined that a man had a perfectly ordinary illness at a time when his defenses were down. You have determined that the blood bank performed exactly as it should have. You have not discovered how he acquired AIDS, and I propose to you that you will do a great disservice to the memory of one of the leaders of our generation if you continue to flog this question. I have devoted a great deal of effort to diverting the public from lurid exposés. That battle is nearly won; Epps is no longer a front-page story. Your persistence in this fool's errand will certainly bring back every muckraker. And I assure you Epps's homosexuality will come to be an accepted fact, whether you and your epidemiological colleagues decide there is proof or not. That will be a major threat to the Epps philanthropies worldwide.

"Beyond that, you will do immeasurable damage to the American health-care system by lending credence to the idea that hospitals can't manage their blood banks. The public is already paranoid about that issue. Your inevitable exoneration of the blood bank will be ignored, and it will take years for the profession to recover from your escapade. Finally, this investigation of yours is sure to get notoriety that neither this hospital nor the rest of the country, nor you, ultimately, can afford."

One more try. "There's really no need for anyone else to know. Dr. Low and I can continue to look into this ourselves, without involving any of our staffs." He looked to Low but couldn't make eye contact.

"If there is more looking into to be done, Dr. Low will

do it. Let me make your position perfectly clear. You have no role in this matter. You and your staff are to stop all activities related to Epps. You will not enter the blood bank or talk to present or former blood bank personnel without my explicit prior approval. I consider this matter closed, and expect you to do the same. Now if you will excuse me, I have other things to attend to. Dr. Low, come with me." They departed through the rear of the office, leaving him alone.

Unfortunately, Larraby's logic and global view of the issues was typically impeccable. And Larraby had clearly been pounding both the facts *and* the table. But Montana was already hooked. Life would have been simpler if he had already stopped at the lab and picked up Epps's month-old tube of leftover blood. On reflection, he decided this was not the time to be overly cerebral. A half hour one way or the other was unlikely to change the world. He made his way against the tide of white coats to lab control.

Lab control was a room twenty feet square attached to a bank of walk-in refrigerators and freezers. The four thousand blood, urine, sputum, and "other" samples that UHOP tested every day went there first to be logged in, sorted out, spun down, and moved along to the appropriate diagnostic laboratory. At this moment, the morning rush was in full swing. Ten people moved gracelessly about the cramped, poorly laid out, inadequately lit room. When one inadvertently looked his way, Montana took him by the elbow.

"I need a red-top tube from about a month ago. Here's the patient's unit number."

"We're pretty busy. I'll look for it later. Put the number on that bench."

"I really need it now."

"You need a four-week-old sample this minute? Those things are all congealed and some of them are moldy. Nobody ever uses them." This was probably true.

"We won't know until you look. I'm sure it will be quicker than taking time off to explain to the Department of Public Health why you can't find any of your sterilizer quality-assurance checks."

The fellow eyed his already-growing pile of unprocessed specimens, took the paper from Montana, and disappeared into the cold room. Five minutes later, he emerged empty-handed. "We don't have it."

"What happened to it?" Montana asked.

"I guess it got thrown away."

"Don't you keep those samples for three months?"

"Yeah, it must've gotten lost. Look, I got to get back to work."

"You mean you have other specimens from that far back?"

"Yeah, some. It happens." The fellow had turned back to his bench. He was about three hundred test tubes behind.

# TWENTY-FIVE

MONTANA loosened the tie, thinking that with a little effort it could be made into a noose. He signed out his beeper to Carola and set out on foot toward Penn. He figured if he walked slowly, he'd get there just about at the end of Molly's lecture to the medical students. She usually introduced the first hematology lecture by draw-

125

ing a parallel between the institution's colors, red and blue, and its history of distinguished contributions to the field of blood research. After a short pause, she asked, sotto voce, "Aren't you glad you don't go to Brown?"

He arrived much too early and went to the University Museum. As a kid, he had watched "What in the World?"—an ancient TV program in which a panel of archaeologists made erudite, occasionally correct, comments about artifacts whose orgins were kept secret from them but not from the audience. Montana retained none of the specifics, but when, as an adult, he first visited the museum, its collections evoked the winter afternoons that a ten-year-old had spent inside a blanket tent pitched over chairs in his living room, watching four men in narrow ties talk about pre-Columbian Central American statuary. He had visited the Museum many times, but when he did so alone, he invariably passed the time sitting in one or another of the dimly lit, sparsely trafficked galleries.

His kids, on the other hand, believed the place to be the wellspring of Saturday-morning cartoon shows about hidden or lost civilizations sequestered deep in impenetrable jungles. They never moved slower than a fast trot when they visited it. It was the source of their favorite pun, which involved going to Penn to see Mummie. Whenever they arrived at her lab or the museum, they insisted they had been taken to the wrong place. The routine had acquired special status after Isaac, saying he was dressing as his Mummie, went trick or treating on Halloween wearing several miles of bandages and a white plaster of Paris life mask of Molly.

For an hour and a half, Montana watched the oversized variegated goldfish in the pool outside the museum's entrance, then set out in search of Molly. He found her in the well of the amphitheater, surrounded by a handful of students who had questions left over from the lecture. She disposed of them and joined him in the back row.

"You run across the strangest people in a place like this," she said, taking his hand as she settled into the next seat. "Are you slumming?"

Montana told her about the blood they had been counting on that wasn't there anymore. And about Larraby forbidding him any more investigation. Then they sat, silent, in the company of physiologists whose larger-than-life-sized portraits hung from the walls, as Montana labored with the probabilities with which they were left, instead of the absolutes this situation required. His world was typically full of shades of gray. Although Molly's hypothesis about intentional blood swapping had the ring of truth, Larraby might actually have been right. Montana's dilemma couldn't have been keener. If he and Molly were right, they would lose—either by remaining silent and knowing a bizarre unexplained murder had been committed or by making the claim publicly and then in all likelihood being sued for libel. If they were wrong, a public claim would end the same way. As events had played out, the only "satisfactory" outcome would be for them to be wrong and not to broadcast any of it. No losers that way, just embarrassed amateurs.

Molly broke the silence. "UHOP is too big to have only one lab that stores blood samples. Epps must have had every esoteric test in the book. Maybe one of those labs freezes its samples."

Together they enumerated the possibilities. The most promising was virology, where CMV studies were performed; but Epps's diagnosis had been made on lung tissue, and there had been no need to do any other diagnostic tests. When the answer came, it seemed they must have been purposely ignoring it. Epps's HIV-antibody test had been done at the Philadelphia Blood Reference Center.

**127**

Montana had started to run to Spruce Street to hail a cab when Molly called him back. "Let's let our fingers do the walking." She seemed unconcerned by his warning that the blood had been submitted under a fictitious name, which he didn't know.

In her office, Montana listened to her side of the conversation with the Reference Center. Only it wasn't Molly Montana, sometime collaborator of the center's director, who called. "This is Dr. Belkins' office. Dr. Belkins needs to have an Rh-antibody test done on a sample he sent you from UHOP about four weeks ago. . . . Well, actually I lost the slip he gave me with the name, but maybe you could help me out. The other girl said it's the only one he sent you. . . . You did an HI-something test. . . . Yeah, HIV, that's it. . . . Right, the patient's name *is* Stetner. The doctor really needs that Rh test result bad. Could you run it this afternoon and call me here? I'm actually at his other office; here's the number."

In subsequent years, Montana found he could remember every minute of the next three hours. By turns, he and Molly paced, sat, stretched, and stared out the window.

At 4:30, the call came. Stetner/Epps had antibody. Not much, but it was unequivocal. There could be no denying that Epps had received someone else's blood; and beyond a reasonable doubt, that blood had been Rice's and had given Epps AIDS. Given UHOP's blood banking safeguards, the switch had to have been intentional. The Montanas silently shared the same abdominal knot.

# TWENTY-SIX

"WE KNOW how he was done in, all we need to do is figure out who and why." Molly's years of watching every cop show on TV put her well ahead. She was heavily into motive, method, and opportunity.

"I give up. Why don't we tell the police?"

"Because they won't be able to tell us from the three hundred cranks who offered them the true, secret, and smarmy details of Epps's last days on earth. You don't expect to tell the first desk sergeant you meet that an unknown person killed Epps for an unknown reason by a method that the cop has never heard of, do you? The best you'll get is a quick escort to the exit. This problem shouldn't be all that hard to solve. If we know who had access to the blood, we can work from there. Who had access to the blood?"

"Adrienne Martinson said she was the only one who handled AIDS blood. She moved away soon after the transfusion. Any idea why she would have done it?" Montana asked.

"Dearest, that's why we discuss these things *before* we talk to the police. Unless she's incredibly smart or phenomenally stupid, she doesn't get on the list at all. She volunteered all kinds of information that would only cook her goose if she was the one. And the reason she gave for leaving is easy as pie to check. If you were going to make

129

up a reason for leaving, you'd pick one that couldn't be verified like that. We better find out if Ru suggested the job to her and not vice versa. Who else was there?"

"There are probably twenty techs who knew the blood was there, but I don't see why any of them would have cared. I also don't even know most of their names, let alone how to decide whether to follow up on them," Montana said. "It also doesn't make a lot of sense; none of them has benefited from Epps's demise as far as I can tell."

"That would be a great excuse, except no one has benefited at all, so far as we can tell. Were there any non-techs?"

"Amos Zenana. He used to pick up infected blood. So he would have known about it and had access."

Molly brightened at the mention of his name. "Now there's a fellow that even a mother couldn't love. He's as mean-spirited, double-dealing, and contemptible as they come."

Zenana was Philadelphia's contribution to the international AIDS research extravaganza. At fifty-eight, he was five feet three inches of the meanest SOB who ever shook a test tube. He had been a bright, energetic, hardworking, moderately successful, if none too pleasant, immunologist in the years B.A. (before AIDS). AIDS was the answer to his prayers, coming when his career had reached a plateau. It brought him more research support than he could shake a stick at and an army of assistants whom he drove relentlessly. He now headed a small AIDS empire. But much more important, AIDS brought him celebrity, a jet-setter's lifestyle, and a chance for a piece of the Nobel prize(s) that would surely be given to those who won, or appeared to win, the race for a cure.

This contest had neither rules nor ethical restraints. Stories of his usurping others' data circulated widely, and were correct. His university's committee for scientific probity assigned a full-time staffer to investigate complaints made about him by employees, colleagues, and other researchers around the world. It was correctly assumed that he would sell his soul, had he not hocked it as an undergraduate at Swarthmore.

Molly continued, "Every time I see that creepy little man, or look into his beady black eyes, or shake his sweaty hands, I say to myself, 'Molly, there's a man who would commit murder as quick as you can say, "complement-fixing antibody."' Montana, that guy would only need half a reason to kill Epps. Do you know any?"

"Not me," Montana responded. "On the one hand, they probably didn't know each other, and on the other, Zenana didn't need Epps's research support. Nothing's changed in Zenanaland since Epps's death. He was a successful arrogant little bastard before Epps died and he still is."

"But he sure does fits the type, and we don't have any other prospects."

Molly was right. Zenana was the only suspect they could muster. They walked, hands in their respective pockets, to Molly's car (parked a mere fifty yards from her lab, a fact Montana still could scarcely credit). Autumn was the best of seasons to sit in traffic. Even mixed with exhaust fumes, the air was crisp and fresh enough to breathe. The sun hadn't yet set, and the traffic cops weren't suffering from exposure and taking it out on the motorists. Best of all, the Montanas had no need for their car heater, which provided both heat and an earsplitting racket. They listened to Terry Gross on WHYY interview an urban planner about his new book *Gridlock*. By the time they arrived at day care, Montana proposed their next step. "We talk to Grace Epps. She needs to know what's going on. And she might know something about Zenana."

131

"And I have been dying to meet her," Molly said. "Wait 'til the girls at work hear that I know Grace Epps."

"Who's gray Sepps?" asked Isaac, who was still patting Foofoo, the rabbit that Molly had donated to the center after rescuing it from the usual fate of lab animals that had made their share of antibody.

"Nobody special," she replied, putting the rabbit back into his cage. "If you and Abe get your things real quick, I'll tell you the story about the doctor who stole dead people's heads and mailed them all over the place until one of the packages leaked and the mailman opened the box."

"Gross," said Isaac.

"Ugh," said Abraham.

They were ready in a flash.

# TWENTY-SEVEN

MOLLY WAS still looking at the well-filled sweatshirt that was driving off with their car when Grace Epps opened the door. "Dr. Montana, I have enjoyed watching you row many times. It is a special pleasure to meet you." She led them through five minutes of pleasantries before arriving at, "How have you fared with your queries, Dr. Montana?"

Montana reminded her of Epps's postop illness and explained that it probably had been the first sign of his

HIV infection. She saw immediately the implications in terms of Epps's having acquired the infection at UHOP. Molly then outlined the Rh system and their use of it to confirm that Epps had received someone else's blood. Mrs. Epps gave no response at all, prompting Molly to ask whether she had followed the explanation.

"I believe so, dear."

"The rest is extremely difficult, Mrs. Epps," Montana rescued Molly. "I've reviewed the blood bank from every possible angle. And I see no way for the blood to have been switched accidentally."

Mrs. Epps raised one eyebrow, an affectation she had shared with her husband.

He continued, redundantly. "Bizarre as it sounds, we think someone must have exchanged the blood intentionally."

"Why is that so 'bizarre,' Doctor? My husband had enemies."

"Ma'am, anyone in a position to make the switch would have known that your husband might never get AIDS from the transfusion, and if he did, it might not be for years."

Grace Epps was not discomfited. "But he *certainly* would develop a positive HIV-antibody test. Have you any idea how many blackmail threats my husband received? Based on nothing but the hope that a very rich man would rather pay than have groundless charges trumpeted about? If you planned to make a claim of sodomy, you might like to know that your prey would have an incriminating blood test, should the need arise."

That was a motive, which was more than the Montanas had managed. "Did your husband get an AIDS blackmail threat?" Montana asked.

"I don't know of any, but I can try to find out."

"The only people who knew about the infected blood

in the blood bank were a myriad of technologists, and Dr. Amos Zenana."

Grace looked up from the notes she was writing in her small leather-bound diary. "Of course I know of Dr. Zenana, although I've never met him. I can't remember why he couldn't serve on the foundation's AIDS advisory committee. He and Van had been classmates at Swarthmore, although I gather they didn't know each other there."

Montana hadn't known Molly, either, when they were undergraduates at Penn, save for their watery escapade.

Grace thought there would be no difficulty in learning about the techs and Zenana. While they were at it, they told her about Adrienne Martinson's sudden relocation to Connecticut, ostensibly at Low's request.

"Doctors, is there some reason you haven't included Dr. Low on your list? Mustn't the director have been in a position to know?"

Montana looked at Molly and she at him. The one turned his palms up; the other shrugged her shoulders. Molly spoke first. "We've known Ru Low for an awfully long time. He's a big fat well-meaning guy without a stitch of ambition. I can't imagine a more harmless fellow."

Prompted by the question, Montana pondered his recent discussions with Low. "On the other hand, he gave me the brush-off when I tried to pursue the blood swap idea, and he brought Larraby down on me like a ton of bricks two days later."

"Well, then," said Grace Epps, "why don't I add him to the list?" Closing her notebook, she folded her hands in her lap and sat in remarkable repose for a woman who had just heard that her husband had been murdered.

"I want you to know how much I appreciate your taking the time and effort to look into this the way you have. I know at the outset you considered this tilting at windmills. And although you haven't said so, you clearly stand to suffer by dint of your efforts. But what you have learned so far is a great relief to me. Are you willing to carry on a bit longer? Since the perpetrator is likely a member of your profession, you two can continue less obtrusively than the police could. And I'd like not to endure the commotion of a public investigation just now, if it can be avoided. Both the Epps enterprises and I will provide whatever help you need."

The Montanas were agreeable. "The only thing we could use in addition to the personnel checks is a baby-sitter. Does your foundation have any on retainer?" asked Montana.

"Alas, no. But I suspect your children might not mind spending some time at the estate here with me. If they tire of me, they can ride, swim, visit the kennel, and conscript the chauffeur for games. The only condition is that they and you call me Grace." She spoke now to Molly. "I have tried without success to persuade your redoubtable husband to use my given name. I fear he is a lost cause. But perhaps it's not too late for you and the children."

"That is a problem of Monty's," agreed Molly. "It hasn't rubbed off on the rest of us, Grace."

"I'm very happy to hear that. Perhaps we can loosen him up a bit. I imagine it will take a few days to get any useful information about the people we discussed. I'll call when there is a report. In the meantime, let me know when you can use my services." She saw them to the door and offered them her warm dry hand in farewell.

On the way home, Montana protested their taking advantage of his innate lack of good ol' boyness. "It's a Montana family tradition," he insisted.

"Don't I know, dear," Molly answered. "If making idle conversation had survival value, the Montanas would have died out thousands of years ago. But don't despair. At the rate you're progressing, you should join the company of sociable men and women on your eighty-second birthday. We'll have a very nice party for you."

They drove most of the rest of the way in silence, Montana thinking that the kids would be in their fifties for that party, and wondering whether he would still be riding them home on his bike.

# TWENTY-EIGHT

THE NEXT development did not come from the army of detectives that Epps enterprises unleashed on an unsuspecting populace. Montana spent his free time pondering the Zenana connection. He made copies of Zenana's articles, looking for some clue among the numerous coauthors. He dropped Zenana's name in conversation at faculty meetings. He even asked Carola and Bella if they knew anything about the man. No luck. And then one evening, as Montana was checking the cartoons in *The New Yorker*, he came upon a photo of the Hathaway shirt man. Seconds later, he was on the phone to his writer friend, Bert Edwards.

"Bert, I'm coming to collect that dinner you owe me."

"Not so fast; you're twelve years early. They haven't even demolished the apartment building where they're going to build the high rise that will house the restaurant where we're going to eat. Show up now and you'll get a hot dog from a pushcart."

"In that case, you come here. I'll meet you at the usual place tomorrow at five." In Philadelphia, everybody met at Wanamaker's eagle. Montana and Bert used the Main Concourse of Thirtieth Street station, a domain supervised by the most somber of angels.

The next day, Montana spotted Edwards, wearing matching madras blazer and patch, as he emerged from the train platform. "So, Mountain Man, what is it to be tonight? Moussaka, tripe, sweetbreads?" Montana couldn't abide sweetbreads.

"None of the above. Did you know poor benighted Philadelphia has an almost decent Indian restaurant? We're going to eat vindaloo until you say uncle, cousin."

"Uncle, cousin. I had to leave my tongue for emergency repairs at the last Indian restaurant I visited. They promised to return it at the end of the year if I agree never to set foot in one again."

"Not to worry. We're going to The Boston Brahmin. They'll serve you codfish cakes if you're too chicken to eat curry."

Edwards eyed Montana suspiciously, then set off on a new tack. "I go nowhere without Molly. She'll protect me from whatever chicanery you have in mind. Anyway, she's the only reason I came to town. You're pretty dull company, in case nobody mentioned it to you before."

"You and everybody else. She's going to meet us there. My traitor of a son, Abe, said I was too boring and insisted Molly give him supper."

They cabbed down to Penn's Landing, Edwards's eye growing rounder by the minute. "God save us from dictators and urban planners. Whatever happened to our nice seedy waterfront? This stuff is regurgitation city. Hey Mon, don't do it. I can take anything but eating in a refurbished sailing ship."

"It's okay. We're going a couple of blocks from here. I just wanted to see how you liked it."

137

They found the Brahmin, a timeless export of the Indian subcontinent. Bare Formica tables, dime-store light fixtures, and wallpaper that affronted every aesthetic sense. Their appetizer of cucumbers and yogurt had just arrived when Molly strode in wearing a pearl-buttoned western shirt, open at the neck to reveal a single silver-chased onyx bead on a black cord, Levis, and cowboy boots. She gave Edwards the hug she reserved for the long lost and those feared dead.

"Didn't you tell me this was a western place? I was expecting to ride the mechanical bull."

Montana looked around the little room. "I guess it's out for repairs. Why on earth were you expecting one?"

"Because when you told me we were going to the 'Brahma,' and I asked you if it had a rodeo motif, you gave me your usual grunt. I feel like a born-again jerk dressed this way."

Bert came to the rescue. "I'm sorry no sari. You're a knockout either way. Tell me what your kids are up to."

"You should have seen the look on their faces when a stretch limo with a chauffeur arrived at the door. By the time they discovered the color TV and a bar stocked with seven brands of soda, even Jaded Jake had lost his cool. Those kids may turn us in for a new model as soon as they get the chance." As an aside to Edwards, she said, "New baby-sitting service. I think Momma could use a little sitting, too."

Edwards was always tough to impress. "I guess the research business is picking up. Have you guys figured out how to make bacteria turn lead into gold?"

"Next year," Montana replied as he chased the last cucumber. "Right now we're frying other fish. Speaking of which, are you really going to have fish cakes?" They settled on a blow-your-brains-out fish dish, a pathetically mild chicken and peanut concoction, and four kinds of bread. Forty-five minutes later, saffron rice spilling from

**138**

their ears, they drank fragrant tea and watched the other Yuppies heading to the waterfront.

Montana asked, "How's your work on Epps going?"

"Nowhere. I found all kinds of tidbits but neither you nor anyone else had anything that would interest the paying public. Anything cooking?"

"Not this minute, but there might be soon. It depends a little on our finding out some things about Epps's old college acquaintances."

"My, my. Who ever would have pegged you for amateur sleuths? Are you taking up my line of work?"

"Nope. You can write about anything we find out that's interesting and won't get us sued for libel."

Molly chimed in, "Monty noticed something he thinks is unusual and he's trying to decide if it's another idle rumor. Think of it as a midlife crisis. Help him out and he'll be your friend for life."

"That's what I was afraid of," said Bert. "If you withdraw the offer, I'll tell."

"Just tell me the part about young Epps's close friendship with a fellow undergraduate."

"What if I tell you that you really don't want to know? This guy is pretty well known. I wouldn't even use his real name in my book."

Montana had more tea. "Are his initials A.Z.?"

Bert leaned forward and raised his eye patch, as if scrutinizing Montana very carefully. "It took me months of work and some serious cash to uncover that morsel. How did *you* manage it?"

"Mostly luck. I found out they had been contemporaries at a pretty small college and so must have known each other. I've been wondering whether there might be any reason for bad blood between them and your remark about Epps's hidden past seemed about right. Even so, it was a long shot. Is there any more to tell?"

"You got most of it. Zenana was a scrappy kid from

**139**

Marcus Hook. He and Epps were inseparable for a year or so until Epps cooled the thing off. Nobody I talked to knew whether it was his own idea or his family's. Zenana was pretty broken up about it; at one point, he threatened Epps. Said he'd tell the world that Epps had seduced him. Epps, being a devil-may-care sort in those days, reportedly didn't much mind who Zenana told what. As far as I know, they didn't have anything to do with one another during their last year in college. I looked hard and couldn't find any evidence of contact between them since then. Happy?"

"Yes, thank you very much. I hope to return your kindness in the near future. Now," he continued, "for your just dessert."

They adjourned to the Montanas' town house, which Edwards hadn't seen, and they waited while he said pleasant things in the general direction of the kids' photos. They put in a solid hour and a half dunking grapes, bananas, and pineapple into melted semi-sweet chocolate. Whimsy camped at Molly's feet and, for his convincing show of affection, received fifteen grapes, six banana slices, and the pot to lick. Montana eventually pried Edwards loose and walked him and Whimsy to the train station.

They returned home to find Molly lying on the living room floor, her face a pale green, her knees folded up to her chest, and her arms wrapped around her middle. "The chocolate and curry are having a war inside here. Do something." Montana sat next to her and rubbed behind her ears. "That isn't helping," she said.

"I know, but it's better than saying 'I told you so.'" To the surprise of both of them, it did help.

After she regained her composure, they surveyed the evening's accomplishments. Molly pointed out that Zenana had increased his lead in the suspects' sweepstakes by a considerable amount. "You couldn't ask for a better motive to go with this method. What a tremendous piece of luck for him. After all these years, he gets the chance to bump Epps off and simultaneously incriminate him for the same sexual behavior he thinks Epps coerced him into."

"Is it time for the cops now?" Montana asked.

"Almost. I think we should talk to him about it first. In case he didn't do it, we'll want to wipe the egg off our faces privately."

Montana agreed to talk to Zenana. Then he called the Epps estate to say they were on their way out to pick up the kids. Grace told them all three kids were at that moment snoring away in one king-sized bed and were planning to have breakfast with her in the morning. Molly and Montana were welcome to join them for breakfast. They accepted the invitation and retired, falling asleep to the sound of Molly's churning stomach.

# TWENTY-NINE

AT 6:30, Molly suggested *she* drive, and when they arrived at the mansion, she handed over the car keys in a remarkable interchange that involved fluttering her lids, shaking hands at length, and *her* holding the door for the chauffeur. It seemed to Montana all she could do to restrain herself from fastening his seat belt. Grace ushered them in, saying, "The boys are helping to groom the horses. They'll be back in a few minutes."

And they were. The little ones swarmed into the dining room, charged to their parents, and started explaining the difference between a stallion and a gelding. Four anatomically explicit minutes later, they came up for air and said, "What's for breakfast?"

The Montanas had kippers, Grace had grapefruit and a croissant, Jacob and Isaac had pancakes, and Abraham had Fruit Loops. The kids believed themselves to have entered a state of grace. Montana didn't even contemplate telling them it was only the house of Grace, until Isaac said, "Grace said we can come back whenever we want. She has a swimming pool and we can use it if we bring our swimsuits. Part of it's inside and part's outside. Did you ever see one like that? And she said we can ride the horses. And she's going to get some video games."

"You mean, Mrs. Epps," Montana interjected.

"No, Dad, she *said* we should call her Grace. It's okay, isn't it, Mom?"

"Yes, dear, Daddy is a little old-fashioned sometimes. Abe, use your napkin. Grace, they may never recover from this overnight."

"I hope not," Grace replied. "The place hasn't been this lively in years. Abraham Rush, Isaac Sayers, Jacob Archer, and I are planning their next visit for this weekend. Will they be free?"

"They haven't used their full names since they visited Santa. What else did they tell you?" Montana asked.

"Many things. All of them to your credit, doctors. I hadn't known your medical roots were quite so deep, Montana. Or that the Montanas intend to start a kennel."

"Fortunately, Molly doesn't hold a person's background against him," Montana remarked. "And the kennel is a figment of overactive juvenile imaginations."

Molly winked at the children and they at her. All four yipped quietly.

The children did not, in fact, have pressing obligations,

and the Montanas agreed to spend Sunday afternoon at the estate. At 7:30, when they attempted to mobilize the kids, Jacob said Grace was going to take them to school in the big car. They drove to town in a bemused silence. Molly dropped Montana at UHOP and continued on, wishing she could have gone to school in the big car, too.

Montana wasn't able to log on to the hospital computer, getting a message instead to contact the system administrator. When he arrived at his office, he found Carola and Bella waiting outside in the hall with a U.S. marshal. The marshal handed him an envelope and left. Montana asked why everyone was standing around so far from the coffee.

"They changed the lock. We can't get in. The guy with the badge said we had to wait for you."

Montana sat on the marble bench outside the office and opened the envelope. It contained a notarized one-page letter from the hospital's legal counsel, which read:

The United Hospitals of Philadelphia hereby relieves you of all professional responsibilities associated with your employment at this institution. You are on administrative leave, with pay, until further notice. Convey all documents and hospital equipment in your possession to Mr. James Dickinson, in the Office of the President. Instruct your staff to report to Mr. Dickinson.

Montana showed the letter to the crew.

"What the hell is this all about?" asked Carola.

"It is about Dr. Larraby's firing me, is what it's about," replied Montana. "He got angry with me a few days ago; I guess he hasn't gotten over it." Montana did not, in fact, think Larraby had been that upset, and if he had been, Montana didn't know why he had delayed all this time.

"After all the times you saved this hospital from itself. That's a hell of a nerve," said Carola. "Anyway, he can't do

**143**

that. You can file a grievance against the hospital." Carola was on the labor committee of the local ASCAP chapter.

"*You* could file one if the hospital did it to you. He can do just about any damn thing he pleases to me. There isn't any doctors' union here, and I don't exist as far as the National Labor Relations Board is concerned. I'm management, you know. All UHOP has to do is fulfill its contract with me, which means pay me until June."

"It's still wrong," Bella protested. "And anyway, that guy Dickinson can't do your job. He can't even do his own. And he doesn't know anything about what we do. I bet the Accreditation Commission won't accept it."

"I'm sure Dickinson doesn't intend to do it at all. He'll just keep you in line until they find a replacement for me. This is all going to be history before the Accreditation Commission ever gets here."

"We'll see who keeps whom in line," said Bella. "Do you know that guy spends full time looking at my chest when he talks to me? Four to one that he spends the next three weeks putting the make on us. Carola, time to pull out that frump outfit you got for your first meeting with Molly. I bet we'll do any damn thing we please around this place as long as he thinks he can get to first base with one of us."

Everything they said was both true and irrelevant. Although a busy stairway wasn't the place for a pep talk, he said, "Folks, they're angry with me, not with you. All you can do at the moment is get yourselves in a jam. The best you can do now is go see Dickinson and promise to be good little girls. Maybe Larraby will cool off."

They left, epithets flying. Montana walked out with them and watched until they rounded the corner. He didn't for a second think Larraby would change his mind. Larraby was notoriously steadfast in his decisions, unless there was an economic or political reason to change them. And neither applied in Montana's case. He didn't bring in big bucks and he had no constituency in the hospital to argue his case. Basically, he was finished at UHOP. One of his namesakes had been denied tenure at Penn, but this was his first ever flat-out rejection, not counting college applications, and he realized almost immediately how disastrous it was. If Larraby was angry enough to kick him out rather than just wait for the end of the academic year, he would probably also make it impossible for Montana to find another job. Certainly not in the Philadelphia area, maybe not anywhere. And anywhere wasn't a real option, since Molly wasn't likely to find a job there. He was suddenly seized with a mental image of Molly adding his death notice to her collection, one more victim of the epidemic of stress they'd discovered.

The early-morning sun gave way to low dense clouds and the temperature dropped precipitously, making the sidewalk an even less inviting site for pondering his fate. Montana made his way around packing crates, vegetable sellers, and pretzel vendors to the subway. Waiting on the platform for a train to take him home to center city, he eyed the panhandlers, mimes, and musicians with a new sense of fellowship. He began to see the appeal of time spent with the crowds in the warm underground stations.

The phone was already ringing when he got home. It was Carola. "Montana, they transferred us. They assigned Bella to do pregnancy tests at the satellite clinic in Chester, and they put me in the gastroenterology lab. I spent the morning measuring fecal fat." She was angry at the beginning and furious by the end.

Montana was more reassuring to her than he believed the situation actually warranted. "Don't get too nerved up or discouraged. Whatever you do, don't quit. I'm sure that's what they want you to do. I think this is a temporary problem. It'll probably work out in a little while. And if it doesn't, we can all move to Trenton." He kept talking until she had regained her composure.

**145**

"Montana," she said, "I think I know what made Larraby so mad. The people in lab control told me that Dr. Low got very upset when he saw an Rh-antibody test report from the Blood Reference Center. He called up as soon as he got it and asked if you had ordered it. He hung up when they couldn't find any record of the specimen at all. They said the funny thing was they couldn't even locate the patient."

"Thanks, Carola," Montana replied. "That's probably it. I don't know exactly why he cares so much about it, but it sounds right. Why don't you and Bella come over for dinner on Saturday? It'll be good to have a chance to get together."

She thought they could, said they would try to stick it out, and hung up. Carola's call got Montana moving again. If UHOP was willing to fire him for pursuing the Epps business, then Low and Larraby must really not want information on the transfusion to get out. This was as close to an admission that the transfusion had been bad as he was going to get. Satisfaction comes in strange ways, he realized. Since he was on forced leave, he could devote full time to Epps.

MOLLY TOOK the news of Montana's sacking with remarkable aplomb. "Darling, I'm sure there will be a great line of hospitals begging you to be their epidemiologist.

The children and I will visit you in Duluth, or wherever, at least once a month." Gallows humor was one of many questionable traits Molly had inherited from her mother. "Better than no humor at all," she once said.

Montana had located the peripatetic Amos Zenana, whose current trip had taken him only to the tip of Long Island, where the Cold Spring Harbor Laboratories were holding a workshop on the conformation of the HIV surface proteins. In the morning Montana delivered the kids to school and then crossed the Ben Franklin Bridge and headed up the Jersey Turnpike. He arrived at the conference shortly after the afternoon session had begun. He penned a note for Zenana, asking if they could meet for a drink that evening, attached it to the message board, and left. Interested as he was in AIDS, he knew that these talks would be entirely unintelligible. He spent the afternoon parked on a dock, watching the seagulls and listening to an oldies rock and roll station. He returned to the conference hall at five o'clock to find Zenana's reply penned on the bottom of his note:

7:30 at the Longshoreman—AZ.

Montana called home, told Molly he'd be home after bedtime, and then had supper at an "all you can eat" spaghetti joint. He found Zenana at the bar drinking Irish coffee. Montana ordered a Beck's and the two moved to a booth that had a bowl of oyster crackers. They already knew each other superficially, and Zenana had neither ability nor interest in small talk.

Montana started right in. "I'm hoping you can help me solve a mystery. I've been trying to determine if Vanning Epps could have acquired AIDS at UHOP."

"Going into the scandal business, Montana?"

"It's a new line of work." Montana realized this was closer to the truth than he would have liked.

**147**

"I can save you some time. The lordly Mr. Epps was a pansy. I can even give you names, dates, places, and identifying marks. Why don't you stage another UHOP press conference and tell the world? Better yet, why don't you write a discreet note to the Epps Foundation and offer not to hold a press conference in return for a modest consideration?"

This wasn't exactly the way Montana had anticipated the conversation proceeding. "Maybe he was, but I like my explanation better. Epps had an autologous transfusion at UHOP the year before he died. On the day before, his blood was stored in the same refrigerator as a unit of HIV-antibody-positive blood that the blood bank was saving for you. I think the units might have been switched."

Zenana cut him off. "Precisely when was that?" he asked.

"June fourteenth of last year," Montana answered.

"Who donated the infected blood?" Zenana went on. He was very much involved in the discussion now.

"Evans Rice."

"Sonofabitch." Zenana pounded his head with his fist. "I spent forever trying to isolate virus from that blood. It set my lab back four weeks. If you find out what bastard switched that blood, you tell me his name and I will personally dismember him." Zenana was furious.

Montana had never seen a man so angry about anything, let alone a laboratory test. He thought it the better part of valor not to ask why Zenana hadn't checked the HIV-antibody test on that unit in his own lab before starting to work on it. Either it had been a stupid move on Zenana's part or it would be a stupid question. He pressed on.

"You didn't know Epps's blood was there?"

"Why the hell should I? Listen, it's no big secret that Epps and I knew each other back in college. But he didn't make it a practice to write me when he went to the hospital. Maybe it's because I stopped sending him get-well cards."

Since Zenana raised the issue, Montana picked it up. "Were you on bad terms?" He tried to be casual.

Zenana jumped. "I hated his guts. He was a holier-than-thou bleeding heart who would drop a friend in two seconds. Once I actually thought up six different ways to kill the guy. It was a great night's entertainment. And they were all a lot more efficient than giving him a transfusion that might not have any effect for years and years."

Zenana had worked himself into a state and had begun to hyperventilate. Montana realized he was unlikely to learn much more, and that if he stuck around, he might end up having to resuscitate Zenana. He thanked Zenana for his companionship, paid for the drinks, and left at a trot.

On the way home, Montana tried to decide whether he had been the object of the ultimate snow job or whether his and Molly's whole theory had just bitten the dust. If it had been a staged performance, it was a marvelous one, but it was certainly within Zenana's abilities to lay out the entire motive and method for the murder solely as a smoke screen. Montana reached no conclusion by the time he returned home.

To his surprise, Molly was neither in bed nor asleep. She was in the kitchen staring intently at the oven and listening to "L.A. Law." She gave him a perfunctory hug and asked, "Well, did he spill the beans?"

Montana gave her a blow-by-blow account of the interview and put forward the possibility that it had been a diverting maneuver. Molly thought not.

"Amos Zenana is capable of anything except admitting that he'd wasted a month of his lab's time studying the wrong unit of blood. He'd rather be convicted of murder. We need another pigeon."

Ding. Fresh hot double-chocolate decadence.

# *THIRTY-ONE*

MONTANA decided Molly was right. But without Zenana, they didn't have a suspect, leaving Montana nothing special to do. He tried to work on a long-dormant research project, but even his beloved microbes couldn't hold his attention. He considered giving the *Philadelphia Inquirer* anonymous tips about scandals and cover-ups at UHOP. Mostly, he contemplated his shattered career. He and Whimsy hung around in the morning, went to the river at lunchtime to watch Molly row, and then hung around in the afternoon. By week's end, Whimsy was on cloud nine and Montana was a basket case.

On the seventh day, they took their customary places on the reviewing stand. Forty minutes past lunch, and no Molly, they drove back toward Boathouse Row. As they rounded the bend under the Girard Avenue bridge, Montana spied her, soaking wet, jogging downriver. She darted to the side as he slowed down near her and he beeped the horn, then, recognizing him, she trotted over and got in.

"Some fucking bastard dropped a boulder on me," she said. She trembled, mostly from rage, partly from the cold, and increasingly from a growing awareness of her narrow escape. "I was heading under the bridge when a rock went right through my stern. The bow went straight up in the air and the shell sank in about six seconds."

"Somebody did that on purpose?" Montana asked.

"Well, some fucking guy in a fucking bandanna was staring over the rail when I surfaced."

"Jesus Christ, let's get the police."

"Let's get my clothes, first."

At PGRC, Montana called the Fairmount Park police while Molly showered and dressed. Two fellows in mirrored glasses arrived in fifteen minutes. They took a pretty mediocre history. "Ma'am, the City police need to take over on this. We'll keep a lookout for this guy in the park, but they'll follow up the rest. We'll get a report to them in about an hour. You should go down to headquarters this afternoon to give them a statement. They'll also have some photos for you to look at."

The Montanas dropped the dog at home and made their way to precinct headquarters, where they waited two hours before meeting a preppy Detective Griffin. He took a much better history. He didn't assume that this was straightforward juvenile delinquency, and was especially interested in Molly's sketchy description of the bandanna wearer.

"Has this happened before?" Montana asked.

"Every couple of years some kids toss stuff at a rower and then run like hell. But no adults. Have you ever seen him before, ma'am?"

"This week when I was rowing, there was a guy on a bike around the statues a couple of days. It could have been him."

It was Montana's turn to tremble. "You mean he was aiming for you in particular?"

"Don't know. I didn't think my rowing was that big a threat to anybody anymore."

"Rowers have more sense than to try to bean a moving target from the bridge. What about your students?"

"None of them's flunking out or that crazy. And I'm not that bad a lecturer."

"Former beau?"

"They send flowers."

Griffin broke up the routine and showed Molly an album of mug shots. "Dr. Montana," he said, "the guy who did this is probably a loony tune who's been scrambled since he left Vietnam. But I really need you to think carefully about whether anyone would have wanted to hurt you."

Molly shook her head.

Griffin persisted. "You can tell me things that won't go beyond this room if you want. I've met professional people like yourself who managed to get on the wrong side of a loan shark. They weren't bad folks, and we helped them."

Molly shook her head.

Griffin again: "There are doctors who write a few prescriptions for controlled substances and acquire a clientele they can't refuse. Are any of your patients angry with you?"

Molly shook her head.

Griffin's last try: "Give it some more thought, ma'am. Sometimes you remember things after a few days. Here's my card. Call me anytime. Nice to meet you both." He gave them a professional, not totally impersonal, smile and showed them out.

Montana erupted in the car. "Why didn't you tell him about Epps?"

"What about Epps?"

"What do you mean, 'What about Epps?' That you figured out he was murdered."

"Except the murderer doesn't know we know. And you're the one who's been making all the fuss. If he did know, he'd throw a rock at you on your bike. This guy's out to lunch like the lieutenant says."

"Unless he's not. I'm not going to wait while this jerk takes another potshot at you or the kids."

"So a guy who just got fired for concocting funny stories will call up nice Lieutenant Griffin and tell him an even funnier one? No dice."

"You're just going to ignore this?"

Molly was quiet for a moment. "Maybe the kids should visit my parents for a while."

At home, they found a message from Grace on the answering machine, saying that it would be helpful if they could get together at their earliest convenience. Please feel free to bring the children.

The announcement of a visit to Graceland evoked a predictable response from the kids. They tumbled out of the car before it stopped and disappeared in three directions. Molly was too preoccupied to notice the new jock-gray sweatshirt with navy lettering.

Grace was pleased to see them. "I have some information that may be useful. Actually, my investigators discovered two items. The first concerns a very old liaison of my husband's." She paused to clear her throat. "It appears that when Van was an undergraduate, he had a very close relationship with Amos Zenana, of all people. I feel rather foolish, after my original claim to you, Montana, but it seems imprudent to ignore the possibility that Dr. Zenana might know something of value."

"I spoke to Dr. Zenana last week," Montana answered. "Zenana was quite adamant about not having any contact with your husband for many years. I believe him."

"I see," Grace said. "I suppose that is reassuring. Still, one marvels at the indiscretions of youth. I thought I knew everything about Van there was to know."

She reflected briefly, then continued. "The other item I have for you concerns Rudolph Low. Around the time of Van's surgery, the Epps foundation had been negotiating with UHOP to endow a blood components institute. It was to include a chair in hematology with fifteen thousand square feet of lab space and research support for

**153**

the indefinite future. The plan was to have the occupant of the chair be the head of the blood bank, presumably with the intent of recruiting a less prestigious person to direct its day-to-day operations. I understand that in these circumstances it is customary for a new institute head to use such positions for junior associates of their own choosing."

"You mean Ru was about to get canned. Did he know about it?" asked Montana.

"Possibly. We, that is the foundation, try to do these things discreetly, but some version of the facts often circulates. You can see, obviously, that this might have given him reason to perceive Van as a threat."

"Poor guy," said Montana. "Works his whole life at UHOP, builds a respectable blood bank, moves the field ahead a little, and stands to get booted on a moment's notice. Life in the ivory tower's a wonderful thing. What happened to the institute? It should be well on the way by now."

"It was deferred. UHOP foresaw a problem getting a zoning variance for the additional lab space. I gather the neighborhood association has periodically been unpleasantly argumentative. UHOP held out some hope of being able to move ahead in the not-too-distant future."

Molly came to Low's defense. "We've both known him for years. I don't believe he was capable of switching the blood, even if his job depended on it."

Montana picked up. "There's something else. Somebody attacked Molly today. I think it might be related—and it really doesn't seem to be something Low could have done."

Grace looked rapidly back and forth between them. Molly looked daggers at Montana. "It's one thing not to tell the cops," he said. "Grace isn't going to think I'm crazy, anyway." He told Grace about the bombardment. She found it entirely plausible.

"My dears, I'm dreadfully sorry. I should have brought in the police long ago. You must give this up immediately. I'll have a security agent accompany each of you and the children and watch your house until things settle down. Don't even think about objecting; I won't hear of it. What other atrocities have I inflicted on you?"

"You aren't responsible for anything," said Molly. "You ought to know, though, that Montana has run afoul of the UHOP administration. He's on permanent furlough." It was Montana's turn to protest.

Their incipient argument was cut short by Grace's musical laughter. "Oh, those little men. I assure you that your job is safe, and that if you don't want it, you can have any job you desire at UHOP or anywhere else. It hasn't been publicly announced yet, but three years ago Van bequeathed one hundred and fifty million dollars to the hospital. They're renaming the bed tower the Epps Pavilion. Just decide how long a sabbatical you want and I'm confident you'll find your job waiting for you."

"I grateful, Mrs. Epps, but I can't accept your help. I started this, and I won't drag you into it."

"On the contrary, my good doctor. I started it and dragged you into it, as you so quaintly put it. Don't worry for a second that there will be any public acknowledgment of coercion. UHOP will merely realize the truth, that it does have need for your services. Now that we've settled that, I think we should get on with supper."

Molly wasn't ready to leave the subject of the investigation, however. She saw that if Grace went to the police with the evidence they had discovered and the information about Low, that the man was done for. She was resolute in her assertion that Low would not, could not, did not murder Epps, no matter how great the provocation.

"Let us just follow up with Low. Give us a week and then we'll hang it up for good," she offered.

Grace accepted, contingent on their agreeing to stay with her on the estate. She pointed out, with some accuracy, that the place was secure against interlopers, that there was plenty of room for them, that it would simplify the deployment of her various bodyguards to accompany them and the children when they went about their activities, and that she would enjoy their company. Molly went off in the limo to fetch Whimsy. She returned with the dog and a new sweatshirt.

# THIRTY-TWO

MONTANA called the blood bank next morning. Low proved to be inaccessible. He was dead. Lorraine told him the night tech had discovered a puddle of blood outside his office when she went to the big freezer in back to get some plasma. She assumed it was a spill from earlier in the day and started to clean it up. When she opened Low's door to get the part that had seeped under, she found him, wrists slashed, deeply unconscious. He died within the hour.

Montana tried to say something appropriate, but all that came was "Poor man." Molly came home (to the estate) when he told her. Grace hadn't left. They picked up the preceding night's discussion. Grace was determined now to go to the police.

Grace's solicitor notified the police commissioner. The

commissioner came, as did his second in command, and his. They listened, they asked, they summoned the head of the homicide unit. After they talked to Grace, they spoke to the Montanas.

A man with a great deal of gray hair interviewed them. "Mrs. Epps told us an extraordinary story, Drs. Montana. She thinks you have proof that this Dr. Low killed her husband by giving him some bad blood. Can you review it with us? We can take your statements right here so you won't have to come to headquarters." They recounted their evidence for the transposed blood, making sure the officers knew to check with the Blood Research Center for confirmation of the Rh-antibody test result. Gray hair was impressed. They also told him of their reservations about Low's role. The stenographer took it all down. Gray hair was noncommittal.

"Doctors, since you've been so involved in this business, I'd appreciate your going through Dr. Low's files. They might mean something to you."

Montana doubted they had anything to contribute but was intrigued by the prospect of being escorted into the forbidden land of UHOP by a cadre of police. They pulled up to the main entrance an hour later. There were three police cruisers—and a media van. Suicide is news, too.

The blood bank was in turmoil. Their vice-president had given the staff a pep talk, and had thoroughly demoralized them. Montana spent a few minutes with them, talking about Low, saying nothing in particular. The police had cordoned off Low's office, and a crew of technicians was photographing, dusting, sweeping, and vacuuming. Bloodstains covered the desk and chair. The officer in charge ushered them in.

"There's not much here to look at. A bunch of books, a two-drawer filing cabinet, and one of those little refrigerators. It all looks pretty straightforward, but maybe you'll find something useful. We're about finished. I'll be outside if you need anything."

The Montanas covered the bloody desk with Low's ample lab coat and started through his files. Molly took the top drawer and Montana the bottom. Molly's drawer was devoted primarily to correspondence with the American Red Cross about Low's computerized blood bank project. Montana found nothing until he got to the "Miscellany" file. Folded in its own envelope inside the manila folder was a photocopy of a letter from the Epps foundation to UHOP, describing the planned endowment of the blood component institute. It had the ragged look of a well-read document. These didn't really change things. Montana had assumed Low had known about the institute, and Low's preoccupation with blood bank automation was common knowledge.

They reported their conclusions to the officer, who wrote it all down and, as an afterthought, showed them a test tube rack of blood samples. It was made of black plastic-coated wire and held forty tubes with bright-red rubber stoppers. The top half of each had a layer of yellow serum that floated above a thin amorphous white plug, under which was a dark red, almost black layer of clotted blood. It looked like a set of miniature parfaits. "This was in his refrigerator, behind the tonic. His staff didn't recognize them. Any ideas?"

Molly pulled out the tubes one at a time, reading the code numbers on the labels. Montana looked in the direction of the rack without focusing. He was silent for a moment, then said quietly that one of those tubes probably held Epps's blood from his last admission.

The policeman started writing again. "How do you know that, sir? There aren't any names on those tubes."

"Those are the racks lab control uses to store specimens. One rack with a sample of Epps's was missing when I checked a while ago. I think you'll find those are the specimen numbers the lab uses, and that one of them is Epps's."

For the first time, Montana admitted to himself that Low might have done it. This only reinforced to him how poor a judge of character he was. He had thought Low entirely incapable of violence at any level. Even Molly, who was normally unerring in these matters had shared this view. Which proved something. Maybe she'd lived with him too long.

"The poor bastard," he said to no one in particular.

# THIRTY-THREE

AMERICA immersed itself in blood. Epps's murder was discussed on every newscast for the next week and frequently thereafter. *Newsweek* made Epps its cover story, under a banner reading 'Bloody murder.' Bert Edwards wrote knowledgeable articles that were always a little sharper than those of his colleagues. The networks ran focus pieces on blood banking. Every hematologist who could utter a coherent sentence appeared on a news program to explain how Epps had died, and why it wouldn't happen again. Radio talk shows became hematology seminars. "Dear Abby" gave more ink to blood than sex. "NOVA" produced a show on hematopoiesis in almost no time. Junior high school students spoke authoritatively of major and minor cross matches. *Antibody* was used in 10 percent of all Scrabble games played during the next two months. Grace became spokesperson for the American Red Cross.

As a consequence of this frenzied discussion of matters hematologic, the public finally understood what made blood dangerous—and safe. For the first time since AIDS had insinuated itself into the national consciousness, most adults realized donating blood was entirely without risk. After years of decline, hospitals and blood banks found themselves with more donors than they could use.

Even nosocomial infections came to be part of the public lexicon. Even more remarkably, the Montanas' investigation into high-pressure deaths among the faculty received a sympathetic reception from the American Association of Arts and Sciences, the NIH, and Congress. A blue-ribbon commission was impaneled to articulate solutions. Montana and Molly testified.

Nor did the Montanas escape the public's attention. They were mentioned in all accounts, and featured in many. They, their kids, and even their dog were lionized. Molly was invited to row for charity in seventeen cities, five of which had only swimming pools. Whimsy was offered a TV show. Montana was offered his old job at the hospital.

# THIRTY-FOUR

WHERE LOTS had happened, nothing had changed. The cardiac surgeons had taken to putting a towel soaked with disinfectant at the threshold of the transplant patients' door to kill germs on the soles of shoes and the wheels of carts. The floors were covered with muddy footprints and tire tracks. "That's how they do it at Stanford," said Mad Dog. Montana loved it.

Montana's team, back from exile, repaired much of the damage done in their absence. AIDS phobia afflicted the hospital in fits and starts. The labs still kept lists of HIV-positive patients on their refrigerator. "That's how they do it at Stanford," Bella and Carola said in unison when they discussed the problem at their staff meeting. Montana loved it.

Mad Dog was refusing to operate on anybody he didn't know to be HIV-antibody-negative. In the preceding week, he'd decided two HIV-positive addicts with endocarditis and wide-open tricuspid regurgitation "weren't good surgical candidates." A year earlier, he would have had them in the OR for a valve job quicker than you could say "Medicaid." Montana didn't love it, but he figured that a life without a challenge wasn't much of a life at all.

Montana visited the blood bank and found the staff depressed beyond words. They were in mourning. As time permitted, Montana had coffee with the staff and lent an ear to their sorrow and disbelief. They had been Low's family. "What do you think, Dr. M?" they asked. Montana said some things were just hard to understand. But he asked himself the same question all the time. So did Molly.

When a black-bordered envelope arrived in the mail, they left it on the mantel, unwilling to open it, unable to throw it away. There wasn't any question about Low's fitting their old hypothesis. Montana realized that in a roundabout way Molly had been right about Epps's being part of the cluster of deaths, though not in a way that either of them had imagined.

He thought about Low at work and at home; in the car and in the supermarket. Especially in the supermarket as he passed the candy section, and again as he watched the automated meat-packaging devices dispensing a continuous stream of plastic shrink-wrapped trays, each bearing a label with the weight and price and grade of meat, in English and in barcodish. In the old days, he had watched for the entertainment value. Now, every bar code he met echoed Low's counterfeit blood-bag labels.

In the blood bank, he fiddled with those labels— without any real purpose in mind. The blood bank's system was even better than the market's. It made legible, waterproof, tightly adherent labels that wouldn't pull off in one piece for love or money. He and everyone else ackowledged Low must have made new labels for the switched units. The duplicate labels themselves were long gone, buried with the blood bags in a municipal dump. Every time he looked at it, Epps's blood bank record looked the same, showing name, rank, and serial numbers of blood received and blood dispensed. No mention of new labels. That wasn't part of the repertoire.

Interestingly, Montana thought, Low hadn't built in a way to know when labels for a unit of blood had been printed. He asked the computer boys. They didn't think it was interesting at all. "Montana," they told him, "you know that labels are made whenever a unit of blood changes bags or when we crossmatch it. Low obviously saw no need to."

"So you'd know if people make duplicate labels," he answered.

"Look," they said, "this is the first time anyone's ever cared whether another label gets made. And it's probably the last. If we add that stuff to the files, every single lookup will take longer and the whole blood bank will slow down. And it still won't keep a wacko like Low from making a new label to stick on somebody else's bag."

True, true, true, and true, Montana realized. But he winced to hear Low called a wacko. And he still didn't entirely believe Low had done it. At some level, Montana was spending time in the blood bank wondering which of the techs might have done it.

At Montana's next meeting with Selma Sloane to work on their postdischarge questionnaire system, he related his conversation with the computer programmers.

"Sounds to me like you asked the wrong question," she said. "You don't really care whether Epps's file kept a record of labels it printed. You really want to know if there's a way to trace the blood bank's transactions. And it wouldn't help much to talk to the blood bank's programmers anyway, since they're applications programmers and transaction records are taken care of by systems programmers. They probably don't know they exist, and if they did, they mightn't have told you, since that isn't what you asked about."

"What should I have asked?" Montana asked.

"You should have asked if there is a master transaction file that logs blood bank activities."

Montana jumped up to go ask.

Selma pulled him back. "Or we can poke around ourselves and see if there is."

Montana's eyes widened. "What do you mean, 'we'?" Montana didn't know much about computers, but he did know that whatever she had in mind shouldn't be possible. "The terminals in the hospital only let you do certain things. You won't be able to do any programming from them. How are you going to use the programmers' terminals in the computing center?"

"We're not going to use any of their terminals. When we set up the file transfer for your little questionnaire system, we did all the heavy development by linking this cute little personal computer of yours to their great big one by telephone. Watch carefully as we dial the secret number and enter the wonderful world of UHOP computing."

She dialed a number from memory (hers, not the computer's) and seconds later, the familiar log-on message of UHOP's computer flashed on the screen. Except instead of displaying the one or two choices available at any of the hospital's terminals (patient lookup, lab results, etc.), this one just waited for a command. Selma typed in a long string of numbers, letters, and symbols, explaining to Montana as she did so that she was moving up in the system architecture. After several minutes of Selma typing alphabet soup and the computer responding with question marks, she maneuvered them into the system's internal audit trail. He watched in fascination as new transactions were added to the list at the rate of about one hundred per minute. Lab tests, X rays, deliveries, discharges, deaths, and more flashed by at a dizzying pace. Watching all of the activities in the hospital like this seemed to Montana like watching an anthill after Abe had run over it with his tricycle. After a few minutes, they left the new transaction stream and started moving backward. They found the blood bank's affairs mixed in with the 100,000-plus transactions per day. It was all there—labels, times, dates, and the makers of the labels, identified by their codes. They even found a label Montana had made when the techs showed him how to use the system. There he was, in glowing green on green, AM7. Twenty minutes later, they made it to the top of the queue. They were six months back in time, many months shy of the date that Epps's blood had been swapped.

"So?" asked Montana.

"So, they don't keep their records around for more than six months. They have to take them off-line eventually, otherwise the system would fill up with outdated records."

"Do they keep the stuff that's off-line?" Montana asked.

"They write it on to tape."

"How do we get it back from tape?" Montana loved to play twenty questions with Selma.

"You go to the head of clinical computing and don't say anything about knowing there's a transaction file or that only the last six months' data is on-line, and you ask how you can recover your transaction."

Montana's eyes widened again. Having watched the woman fly, he was astonished to hear he had to walk the rest of the way.

# THIRTY-FIVE

EARTHBOUND and hating it, Montana ran to Clinical Computing. He burst in on the head of the shop, Dr. John Quill, an out-of-this-world physician who had taken refuge from clinical medicine and started the system back in the days before video games. Montana explained that he needed to see whether an employee who had contracted hepatitis had handled a contaminated unit of blood.

"Well," Quill mused, puffing on his pipe, "I'd like to help you out Dr. Montana, but reloading those tapes is a big job. We'd have to empty out one of our machines on to tape and reload it with the stuff on the tapes you want. That's a couple of days' work, and some departments would be without any computer support while we did it. The only time we've done it was when the rate-setting commission threatened to take back a month's worth of reimbursements. I'd need authorization from administration to do it." With that, his eyes lost their focus and he returned to his own world. Montana wondered what was in the pipe.

Montana tried to see Larraby that day—without success. He made it in three days later and told him what he really wanted and why. Larraby listened sympathetically to his pitch.

"Dr. Montana, you've been under tremendous pressure, and we've all learned from you the personal danger of such stress. You need to relax and come to grips with the fact that this story is over, and that you and your family are safe. Even if it was a realistic possibility, I'm not convinced that shutting down a central computer and continuing your quest would be therapeutic. It's out of the question to bring down a central computer so you can satisfy a whim."

Gracious as ever, thought Montana. His last try was the police. He saw the police inspector with whom he'd worked and he explained his idea one more time. He told him that they could nail this down once and for all, because the record of the new label was the smoking gun. He got back a pleasant, somewhat vacant stare. Perhaps there was no smoking gun, but there were plenty of powder burns, and they were all over Low. The police department saw no need to reopen the investigation.

Montana found Selma and told her he'd struck out. He explained about having to unload a machine to get the old files back.

"They actually call that kind of archive a dump," she said. "They just dump the information to tape and hope they never have to look back."

"What do we do now?" he asked.

"What do you mean 'we'?" she replied.

"I'm hoping you have another smart idea. Can't you call up and do something?"

"Nope."

"What if I got hold of the tape for you? Could you read it on another computer?" he asked, wondering how he'd get the tape if she said yes.

"It would have to be a machine exactly like the one in central computing. That means not only the same make and model but one with the same amount of memory, and the same directories and the same shell files. It takes weeks to get one of those things up and running, even if you know where you're going. Which we really don't."

"You mean it has to be done on that same machine? Period, the end?" She nodded.

"Have I asked all of the right questions?" he asked. She nodded again.

That night, Montana and Molly discussed the bad news. "Do you think I should keep going?" he asked. She thought he should.

"Is it a big enough deal for me to lose my job over again?" he asked. She thought his job was pretty secure, and did he have in mind what she thought he did. He allowed that he probably did. She said why didn't he go ahead then and hope for the best. She thought Ru was probably looking down on them from heaven and urging him on.

Within twenty minutes, Montana had gotten Selma over to talk to them. He gave her the last slice of the pizza and popped the question.

"How long would it take you to restore the tape we need, if I got you access to UHOP's computer?"

She thought for a while. "About eight hours, I guess. Did they give you permission?" She seemed surprised.

"No, actually I'm planning to do it at night. Would you do it if I can get you in?"

"Are you serious?" she asked. "You'd have to stage a commando raid on the computing center. There are two operators there all night. They're not going to let us play with their toys."

"I promise not to shoot anybody. What do you say?"

The next day was a Friday. Montana called A.N. "I need a favor," he said, and without waiting for a reply, he carried on. "Tomorrow night, you shouldn't be

**168**

available to anyone from UHOP. Not by phone, not by messenger, not by pony express, not under any circumstances."

Montana imagined her gray eyes studying him. After a remarkably short time, she said, "I have plans for tomorrow. We haven't talked." And she rang off.

# THIRTY-SIX

AT ELEVEN o'clock on Saturday night, Montana and Selma strode into the computing center. Selma knew the place; Montana had never seen it. Montana found the operator in charge and gave him a letter signed A. N. Crowe. It read:

> This letter authorizes you to take the computer maintaining the clinical laboratories out of service and allow Dr. Montana to use it to retrieve archived information. It is essential that I have this information by the end of the weekend in order to prepare a briefing paper for Dr. Larraby's presentation in Washington next week. Dr. Montana has arranged for Ms. Sloane to do the work in order to minimize interference with your activities. Please assist him as necessary.

Montana was confirmed in his surmise that they had no idea what Crowe's signature looked like. The first operator talked to the second operator. They called their supervisor, who called the technical director of clinical computing, who called Quill, who called Crowe, whose whereabouts were unknown. "Doctor Montana," they said, "we've never had a request like this before."

"And I hope you never do again," he said. "This is one of those emergencies that you can't plan for. Now, can you tell Selma which machine she should use and point her to your tape archive."

And they did. The operators showed them one that had a nameplate on it reading "Doc." Selma got to work immediately, starting to offload a big chunk of its memory. The operators stood by, watching nervously. Montana watched for about twenty minutes and then toured the facility. The main room was brightly lit, with cables crisscrossing the floor and dropping from the ceiling. There were six other big machines, each a replica of the one Selma was working over. Each had a sign: GRUMPY, SNEEZY, BASHFUL. . . . Montana went back to watch Selma.

Three hours later, she finished offloading and began to restore the data from the time of Epps's first transfusion. It took another three hours to get it up, including the time it took to find the tapes they needed. By five on Sunday morning, Selma had "Doc" eating out of her hand. Once she got things in order, she wrote a little program to strip the blood bank's activities out of the transaction file. At six, she redirected "Doc"'s output to a line printer and asked him to tell all.

For the next hour, they watched as four hundred lines per minute spewed out of the printer and sheet after sheet of continuous form paper folded themselves neatly in a heavy-duty-wire catch basket. They could follow the dates of the transactions as they were printed, and when they got to the day the bloods had been switched, they held on to the sheet, letting all of the following ones fall to the floor in front of them.

Selma found it first. Montana heard his pulse pounding in his ears as they pieced out the columns of the record. As he expected, there were two new labels in a row, one for Epps and one for Evans Rice, the donor of the contaminated unit. They had been printed at 10:30 P.M. from a terminal in the back of the blood bank.

They got to the maker of the labels last.

RL6.

Montana's stomach turned over. He let Selma take the paper, kicked his feet free of the pile that had grown around their legs, and sat down on an out-of-service console.

He called Molly. "Ru did it."

Long silence at the other end, then Molly said, "Well, you owed it to him to find out for sure. Oh, damn."

# Epilogue

FOUR MONTHS later, the Montanas arrived at the Epps's mansion. As they got out of the Civic, Molly's buddy whistled at her slinky full-length beaded black gown, and she whistled in turn at his full-dress livery. They were the among the last to arrive for the reception in honor of A. N. Crowe's installation as UHOP's new president. It was the social event of the Philadelphia season. Montana and Molly received an ovation as they entered the room (the crowd was already standing). The chairman of UHOP's board shook their hands, as did the mayor.

Molly was even more radiant than usual. She introduced the Chairman to Bella and, when the quartet took a break, to Carola. She also dragged Bert Edwards out from behind a stand of potted palms to meet the mayor.

"Well, my friends," said Crowe to the Montanas during a quiet moment in the library, "I had envisioned a different end for us all, when you started your last round of high jinks. I never did hear what made you suspect Larraby."

"We didn't," said Molly.

"Nothing," clarified Montana. "Molly and I thought there was a fifty-fifty chance it would be Low, but our second choice was one of the several dozen lab techs."

"We figured one of them would have been connected to someone who had a grudge against Epps and had taken the opportunity for revenge or blackmail or who

172

knows what." Molly had picked up the narrative, only to relinquish it.

"When the computer gave us RL6, I assumed it was Low. I was dumbfounded when I checked the roster of computer codes and found that RL6 was Larraby."

"But, Montana," Crowe edged a word in, "by the time you called me on Sunday, you had it all put together. You knew his motive and had proof and he had confessed."

"Well," Montana replied, "a lot of things fell together once we started to think about him as the murderer."

"Grace already told us that UHOP had been the only beneficiary of Epps's death, and Larraby would have known about the bequest. That provided a motive," said Molly.

"Since Selma and I were still putting the computer back in working order at that point, it wasn't a big deal for her to get into the accounting system. She unraveled the whole case with her keyboard. The hospital's endowment had been systematically siphoned off to support general operating expenses. It had started about four years ago, with small amounts of money moving across. Larraby certainly would have been able to restore those if the government hadn't changed the reimbursement formulae for hospital care. Instead, the problem got much worse. By the time Epps was hospitalized, about twenty percent of the endowment had been used. Even if he'd been able to keep juggling the books, he would have had to stand by and watch UHOP become a big urban hospital falling apart at the seams. The whole business would have bottomed out in three or four years."

Molly selected a canapé from the tray that was offered. "His dilemma came clearly into focus just about the time Epps was hospitalized. By coincidence, Larraby had led a delegation of visitors around the hospital then. Low demonstrated the blood bank system for them and also showed them the HIV-positive blood when the con-

*173*

versation turned to research on AIDS. Larraby realized that if Epps were to die prematurely, the bequest would solve his problems. At some level, he probably really did justify this as service to the greater good. It's hard not to think, though, that it also saved him from life as an also-ran administrator of a second-rate hospital. Or no life at all, if he'd been cut from the same cloth as his faculty, who tended to take their own lives rather than someone else's."

"All he had to do," Montana picked up, "was keep the enterprise from collapsing long enough to collect. That was one of the reasons he was so conciliatory to the unions when they threatened to strike over the AIDS precautions. The hospital would have gone under at that particular moment if they had walked out for even a few days. It also explained why Larraby was so adamantly opposed to any questions about the role of the blood bank in the whole mess. At the beginning, he was probably just worried that any implication of negligence on the part of UHOP might jeopardize the will. Somewhere along the way, he probably learned about the transaction files. Those tapes were effectively out of his control because he didn't have a way to get to them without attracting a lot of attention."

"So Low became an unwitting accomplice and a pathetic victim," continued Molly. "It was easy for Larraby to get Low to run interference for him because he could present the issue to Low as an attack on Low's precious blood bank."

"Larraby," Montana explained, "was actually the one who prompted Adrienne Martinson's transfer to Connecticut, on the grounds that the fewer knowledgeable people who were around, the better off he was. He also held up the negotiations for the blood components institute, and made sure Low was aware of it, so that he could use it as a threat against him. Poor Low was suckered in so far that he was eventually even willing to steal Epps's old blood from Lab Control when Larraby told him it was the only way to keep his blood bank computer system from being blamed for a transfusion mix-up. Low knew the system couldn't have done it, but Larraby convinced him there weren't any other choices."

Molly went on, allowing Montana to eat the jumbo shrimp he'd been waving around for ten minutes. "Once the other tube of blood was tested at the Blood Research Center, though, Larraby realized he'd have to change tack. The easiest way out was to make it look as though Low had done it to keep his job. Over the course of a few weeks, he broke Low's spirit by telling him he was convinced that the computer system had caused the problem, that he intended to disassemble the whole thing, and to notify all of the regional Red Cross offices that had contracted to use it. Larraby pushed Low over the edge by telling him UHOP was going to proceed with the blood components institute after all. Low would have been unemployable after Larraby publicized the failure of his computer system. Low had no recourse since Larraby continued to remind him that he had committed a felony by stealing the blood from Lab Control. And anyway, he didn't have a clue as to Larraby's reason for deserting him like that. The whole thing played into his mass of insecurities. Larraby guessed correctly that Low would crack eventually."

Montana jumped back in. "As an insurance policy, though, Larraby hired a local thug to drop that rock on Molly, to get us to give up our snooping around. As it happened, he needn't have done that since Low's suicide tied it all into a pretty neat package for him. Larraby was off the hook personally and UHOP was solvent. He could even get Grace off his back by rehiring me and claiming he thought I was doing a good job all along, except for some procedural matter, harrumph, harrumph."

175

Crowe had the good breeding to stand still for this dialogue, most of which covered things she already knew. She was rescued by a waiter who came looking for Montana.

"Can you take the phone, Dr. Montana? It's a Dr. Maddock. It's something to do with leeches."